# A REWARD FOR

## *Jerry*

by

## *Grace Rice MacMullen*

SWORD of the LORD
PUBLISHERS
P.O.BOX 1099, MURFREESBORO, TN 37133

Printed in U. S. A.

# DAVID

Who made all little boys
dear to me, and who is himself dear beyond expression.

## CHAPTER I

Jerry

JAM, peanut butter, pickles, apple, banana, and a loaf of bread — Jerry balanced them expertly as he slammed the refrigerator door with his knee. Just as he reached the kitchen table the apple fell off and rolled under the table . . . but that didn't disturb Jerry in the least. One wipe of a sleeve and it was as good as new. He took a huge bite to prove it, then set about making a sandwich, in a business-like manner. Jerry's mind wasn't on the sandwich, though. While his hands were busy, his mind was also busy with plans for spending this bright March Saturday.

Jerry was eleven ("Going on twelve," he always said), with black curly hair and brown eyes. He wasn't big and he wasn't little, just middle-sized. He went to Whittenburg Grade School and school wasn't so bad — but Jerry lived for Saturdays, as any sensible boy would, when he could do what he wanted to. Now that it was warming up, Saturdays would be more fun than ever.

"Could go swimming," Jerry thought, "Only Mom said not to. Good night, I don't know why not! Just 'cause it's too cold for her, that's no sign Hurry and I couldn't have lots of fun!"

Two bites left half a sandwich where there had been

a whole one, and Jerry was thoughtfully eyeing the Sunday cake his mother had just made, when a sound like a hurricane came from the front porch. Any grown-up would have jumped a mile, then run for cover, but a hurricane was nothing new to Jerry. His best friend, red-headed Timothy Watson, was called "Hurricane" (Hurry for short, they always explained) with reason. Wherever Hurry went—although he was about three inches shorter than Jerry and much lighter—he made an impression. Things crashed and fell loudly, when Hurry went through a room; chairs were pushed and broken and smashed. Hurry didn't intend to spread destruction, however; he was just always in a hurry, and objects always got in his way.

"I'm in the kitchen," Jerry yelled.

"That ole porch furniture—turns over if you just look at it," muttered Hurry, as he pushed through the kitchen door, leaving it swinging wildly. "Hey, Jerry—what're we going to do today?"

"Mom wants the lawn mowed—but I guess that can wait a while. What do you want to do?"

"I thought maybe we could go swimming, Jerry. Had you thought of that?" Hurry helped himself to a banana.

"Aw, I dunno if I want to go swimming." (Jerry liked to make his own decisions.) "It's a little cold for swimming, isn't it?" He managed to shiver a little.

"Cold? For girls, I guess. It sure isn't too cold for me."

"I guess it isn't too cold for me, either—I just thought maybe . . . Say! I know what, Hurry. Let's build a clubhouse!"

"What do we want with a clubhouse?" Hurry swallowed the last of the banana and continued. "Can't swim in a clubhouse—nor play ball, neither."

"Course not, Hurry, but there's lots of things you **can** do in a clubhouse."

Hurry was skeptical. "Like which?"

"Like . . . well, hold meetings, f'rinstance, and plan things, and—oh, all sorts of things!" Jerry tried to show an enthusiasm he no longer felt toward the whole project.

"Huh—doesn't sound like much fun to me. Besides, where'd we build a clubhouse?"

"Oh, I don't know. That was what they did in a story I read the other day, and it sounded like fun."

"My goodness, Jerry—you have to be reasonable! In the story they had some lumber, didn't they?"

"Yeah."

"Well, we haven't. We haven't even got a place to build a clubhouse. No, sir, I figure the thing for us to do is to go swimming. Come on, let's go!"

"Well, I **might** want to go swimming," Jerry considered. "I just haven't decided yet."

"Tell you what; you can decide as we're walking down toward the dam. C'mon!"

And the restless Hurricane, having stood still as long as he could stand it, darted toward the back door.

"Well, good night!" Jerry muttered helplessly, as he fell in behind.

"Race you to the old willow," Hurricane challenged, and Jerry broke into a run. By the time they reached the willow tree they were panting, and the sun felt hot and good on their backs. It was a beautiful day—no question about it. Jerry felt a little funny inside. He kept remembering what Mom had said about not swimming until it warmed up some more. But he hadn't really decided to go swimming yet, he told his conscience—and even if he did, Mom just didn't realize how warm it was. Might as well make up his mind to enjoy it, anyway. Suddenly he realized Hurry was yelling at him—from a log placed like a bridge across the river.

"Hey, Jerry, look! How do you reckon this log got here?"

"Don't know, Hurry. Is it strong enough to hold us both?"

"Sure it is. Come on out—careful right there at the edge, though."

Jerry tested the log with his toe . . . and it wiggled alarmingly. "Maybe I'd better not, Hurry. It doesn't look very strong to me."

"Jerry Thomas, are you going to be a sissy?"

That was enough for Jerry. After all, a fellow couldn't be a sissy! He didn't stop to think after that—just went right out on the log. Fortunately it did hold him. It wobbled a little when he stepped on it, but after the first step it seemed strong enough. It was really fun—he felt sort of like the tight-rope walker in the circus as he held out his arms for balance and placed one foot carefully in front of the other. He made a game of it, counting the steps out to the center where Hurry was. A sudden lurch of the log told him that Hurry, impatient with his slow progress, was jumping up and down to hurry him along.

"Hurry! Cut it out! You'll make me . . . "

Whatever Jerry had been going to say was taken right out of his mouth by a wave of brown, muddy water, and the sentence ended with a splash for an exclamation mark. The water was shallow and after a brief struggle Jerry came up, spitting and splashing and shaking his head like a wet, shaggy dog.

"Aw, Jerry, I'm sorry. I didn't intend to knock you off —I was just going to bounce a little."

Jerry shivered. "Whoosh! That's all right, Hurry. I know you didn't mean to do it. Well, give me a hand, will you?"

"Sure. Maybe you'd better wade over to this bank, Jerry."

"This water's c-c-colder than it looks, Hurry, believe me! Specially when you get in so quick!"

"That's just because you're not used to it, Jerry."

"Maybe so." Jerry wrung about a gallon of water from his clothes just by smoothing his hand over his shirt and trousers. "Might as well go swimming now, Hurry. I'm soaked!"

"O. K. The big hole is just around the next bend . . . if we run it'll keep you from getting too cold, maybe."

Just then they heard steps and looked up to see Mike Spann, the scoutmaster, grinning at them.

"Hello, boys. Jerry, aren't you rushing the swimming season a little?"

Jerry looked a little embarrassed, but since Hurry didn't say anything he explained, "Hurry and I were standing on that log and we had a little accident, I guess you'd call it. Anyway, I landed in the water."

Mr. Spann looked a little concerned. "Aren't you afraid you'll catch cold, Jerry? Better come up to the Scout cabin and let me give you a blanket till your clothes dry."

"We're going swimming up by the dam, Mr. Spann. He won't get cold," Hurry interrupted.

Mr. Spann still looked rather stern, and Jerry wondered if he had guessed what Jerry's mother had told him about going swimming. "Well, that's up to you, of course. It is quite cool, still, —and I hope you'll be careful if you swim up there. There are lots of rocks there by the dam, and you really need to know the place pretty well to be safe."

"We'll be careful, Mr. Spann," Jerry said with an assurance he didn't feel. He still felt as though Mr. Spann knew what Mom had said, and didn't want him to go swimming.

"Bye, Mr. Spann—see you Thursday," Hurry said jauntily. "C'mon, Jerry, before you freeze to death!"

Hurry seemed glad to get away from Mr. Spann, even though he was one of their best friends. Jerry realized, surprisingly, that he felt relieved, himself, when they were around the bend and couldn't see the tall scoutmaster any longer. In another minute trousers and shirts had been left on the bank. Jerry did feel better after they got in the water, and he and Hurry had so much fun playing water tag he almost forgot what Mom had said that morning. Both boys were beginning to get tired from all the running and swimming they had done,

so the tag game petered out. Hurry was floating leisurely near the shore when Jerry remembered the "dunking" he had gotten when Hurry bounced him off the log. "Serve him right if I just held him under," he thought.

In two strokes Jerry was across the stream, and Hurry was under water before he had time even to look surprised. Jerry grinned, saying to himself, "And that for ducking me!" Hurry grew so still Jerry decided he must be up to something, so he let go and swam quickly away. There was no movement in the spot he had left, and just then out of the corner of his eye Jerry saw Hurry come up out of the water about ten feet away. "I'll get you now," Hurry shouted from the bank, and dived in head first.

Jerry's mind told him to say, "Look out for rocks!" but

his tongue didn't have time to make the words before Hurry splashed into the water. A sudden alarm went through Jerry. Instead of striking out swimming as he always did, Hurry lurched crazily and then flopped over. The water rippled over him but there wasn't a movement of the floating red-headed figure. By the time Jerry reached Hurry he realized something was wrong—and mighty wrong. He swam as fast as he could to where Hurry was. Treading water, he got Hurry's head up. Then, with quick strokes he pulled his friend to the shore, stretched him out on the ground, and felt for the pulse in his wrist. Jerry's own heart was beating loudly enough; he couldn't seem to find any pulse at all in Hurry's limp arm. In terror Jerry thought, "Four miles from town!" He didn't know whether he should leave Hurry or not, and yet he knew in his sinking heart that there was nothing he could do. "Funny," he thought— "Never realized when we were talking about artificial respiration that I'd ever need to use it. How was it, now?" Jerry made a few fumbling movements, but Hurry was such a dead weight it scared him and he decided he'd better run for help. As he threw his wet shirt over his head, his mind was tumbling with worry. Where could he find somebody quickly, Jerry wondered . . . and all the time that little sick feeling was inside—it wouldn't have happened if he'd done right! Jerry wondered if God would help him, since he was in a mess because of his own fault. He didn't seem to know God too well. Mr. Spann, the scoutmaster, always seemed to have a personal acquaintance with God.

## CHAPTER II

Mrs. Thomas

SUDDENLY Jerry froze. Mr. Spann! Of course, that was where he could get help! Why hadn't he thought of it sooner! If only Mr. Spann were still at the Scout cabin — that wasn't too far away! Jerry threw on his wet shirt and broke into a dead run. Seemed like there had never been so many trees in the trail . . . so many limbs under foot. In many places the ground was still mushy and wet, but Jerry hardly knew it. There was the clearing and the Scout cabin! He banged on the cabin door, shouting, "Mr. Spann! Mr. Spann!" He was so relieved when the door opened and he saw Mr. Spann that he could hardly stop saying it. His teeth were chattering by this time, but he did manage to say, "It's Hurry—he's hurt. Come quick!"

Mr. Spann wasted no time. He grabbed the First Aid kit and set out quickly in the direction Jerry had come from.

"Where is he, Jerry—at the dam?"

"That's right," Jerry panted. "He's—he doesn't seem to be breathing, Mr. Spann."

"What in the world happened, Jerry? Hurry's one of the best swimmers in the troop."

"Yes, sir, but we were fooling around and he dived . . .

I think maybe he hit a rock . . . anyway, he just turned over and I had to pull him out."

Mr. Spann's long strides were steady, and it took all the strength Jerry had to keep up with him. His face was serious, and Jerry thought, "He's as worried as I am."

"Jerry, it might be a good idea to pray, as we go along. I'm not sure I'll know what to do to help Hurry."

"Yes, sir." Jerry was concerned, but he knew Mr. Spann would know what to do. He always did. Still, it couldn't hurt to pray about it . . . they certainly did need God.

"Dear God," he said, way down inside himself, not out loud at all, "Please help Mr. Spann to know what to do, and make Hurry all right . . . And say, God, . . . I . . . I'm really sorry." His heart felt a little better after that, but he was still scared all over as they came up to the dam and saw Hurry still lying as he had left him. Mr. Spann knelt quickly over Hurry, and Jerry couldn't help thinking how he looked as if he knew exactly what to do. Mr. Spann began artificial respiration, Jerry counted silently with Mr. Spann: "One, two, rest. One, two, rest." In, out, in, out, in, out . . . it seemed an hour since Jerry had pulled Hurry out of the water. In, out, in, out . . . suddenly Mr. Spann stopped, waited a moment, and Jerry's heart did a flip-flop as he saw Hurry's chest rise and fall. He was breathing, all by himself! Jerry felt weak all over. But still, Hurry hadn't opened his eyes. Mr. Spann was looking at Hurry's forehead.

"Guess you're right about that rock, Jerry. He's got quite a bump there. That's why he's not conscious yet."

For the first time, Jerry noticed the blood beginning to ooze from a cut over Hurry's eye. Mr. Spann took disinfectant from the First Aid kit, swabbed the cut with cotton soaked in the bright liquid, and then skillfully taped it together. Then he took a tiny capsule from the case, put it in his handkerchief and crushed it, and held it to Hurry's nose as the pungent smell came out.

"Ammonia. It ought to help. Good to have a First Aid kit, isn't it?" Mr. Spann said, watching Hurry's white face very carefully. Jerry couldn't answer. He was thinking about how terrible it would have been if he hadn't found Mr. Spann . . . how Hurry might have died, even . . . how he still might . . .

Suddenly the eyelids flickered, and Hurry's blue eyes stared at them. He blinked again, then a weak smile pulled up the corners of his mouth.

"Hi, Mr. Spann. What are you doing here?"

"Hi, Hurry. Pulling you out of a bad spot, if you want to know it. You gave Jerry and me the scare of our lives, young man."

"What happened, Jerry?" Hurry asked. "I dived in to get you back for ducking me, and that's all I remember."

"You hit a rock, I reckon, and knocked yourself out," Jerry explained.

"Yeah, but — how'd Mr. Spann get here?"

"Jerry ran to the Scout cabin to get me, Hurry. Good thing we got here when we did . . . You were out cold."

Hurry sat up, rather slowly, for Hurry. He didn't seem any too eager to stand up. "Whew! Maybe it isn't such a good day for swimming, after all."

Mr. Spann smiled. "I could have suggested that a little earlier in the day, but I had the impression you had your mind pretty well made up, Hurry. Now, the question is, how are we going to get you back to town, young man?"

"Don't worry about me," Hurry said valiantly, as he stumbled to his feet. "I'm all right." He lurched, and made a wild grab at Jerry. "That is, I'll be all right in a minute, I mean."

"Think you can make it by walking, Hurry? Jerry and I could get a blanket from the Scout cabin and make a stretcher, you know."

"Aw, I can make it, Mr. Spann." Hurry looked rather tired and a little uncertain, but his red-headed determinnation was still there. "That is, if we don't go too fast and maybe rest once in a while, I can."

"O.K." Mr. Spann said. "Get your clothes on, fellow, and let's get back as quickly as we can, and get you warm. Here, Hurry, lean on me a little, when you get tired."

It wasn't the quickest trip they had ever made from the woods back to town, but it was probably the quietest. Hurry had to use all his energy just to walk . . . and Jerry was thinking about everything that had happened. Mr. Spann was probably thinking, too, though Jerry didn't know what he was thinking about. He still felt funny about it; he felt Mr. Spann knew they shouldn't have gone swimming, and was sorry about it. When they came to Jerry's street, Mr. Spann said,

"Hurry's going to be all right, Jerry. We'll get him home and in bed for a few hours to rest up, and he'll be as good as new. I think you'd better scoot on home and get warm, too. Your clothes were already cold and wet. I only hope you don't have pneumonia!"

"All right, sir . . . And Mr. Spann, thanks so much!"

"That's all right, Jerry. See you Thursday, as usual."

* * *

Jerry knew things would be pretty bad when he got home—but he was surprised when he found out **how** bad. Mom would be upset, he knew—disappointed in him, and she'd probably give him just what he deserved—a good spanking. She looked tired when he came in, and hurt. That was something he hadn't expected. It made it hard to tell her he'd gone swimming but he did. Then he told her what had happened to Hurry, too, much as he hated to do it.

"You see, Jerry," his mother said calmly, "That's what happens when one person does wrong. It always makes it hard on that person—and hard on other people, too. Hurry probably wouldn't have gotten hurt if you'd done right—and I wouldn't have spent an anxious two hours waiting for you to come back."

Jerry's lips were trembling by this time, and maybe his mother knew he felt bad enough, without a "licking". In fact Jerry almost thought he'd feel better if she'd spank him and get it over! But maybe she knew that, too—as mothers often do.

A few minutes later, Jerry, in clean, dry clothes sat by the kitchen stove and shivered. His mother dished up a bowl of hot soup and put it on the table, got a tablespoon from the drawer, and added a stack of crackers to the plate. Jerry eyed the meal doubtfully. The soup

looked good—and certainly he was hungry enough—but somehow he didn't feel exactly like eating. That uneasy feeling was still inside. He looked at Mom, bustling round the kitchen as she always did, and the uneasy feeling inside him swelled up and nearly choked him.

"Mom . . ."

Mom didn't look around, just kept right on with what she was doing, but she did answer him. "What is it, Jerry?"

"Mom—I'm awfully sorry about . . . about all this . . ."

The busy hands stopped, and Mom smiled a little as she looked at him.

Jerry continued, gulping: "I know I shouldn't have gone—like you told me this morning—and if I'd done right that wouldn't have happened to Hurry."

Mom came over and put a hand on his shoulder. "I'm glad you said that, Jerry. Makes me feel a lot better!"

Jerry noticed that he felt better, too . . . and my, but the soup smelled good! He grabbed the tablespoon and found the hot soup tasted just as good as it smelled.

"I'll tell you, Jerry," his mother said, "You'll find that Hurry is an impulsive boy—he does things without thinking, sometimes. So you'll have to try to think for him, and keep you both out of trouble."

Jerry thought that over . . . "Guess you're right about that, Mom. Good night, I wish I could do better! I don't know how I get into all these messes, Mom. I sure don't intend to."

"I know it, Jerry. It's what we call our sinful nature. You know that's just what we had in our Bible reading last week. It always has been easier to do wrong than to do right, ever since Adam and Eve in the Garden of Eden."

"That's funny, Mom—but you're right. Why is it, anyway?"

"It's just because we're all human beings, and ever since Adam and Eve sinned, we've been a sinful race of people. That's why God had to send His son, Jesus, to die for us, Jerry."

Jerry was a little embarrassed, and he went on eating soup so he wouldn't have to say anything.

"You know I've always prayed for you, Jerry. I want you to trust Christ, and be a Christian like your father and I are."

Now Jerry really was embarrassed, but he had to say something. "Thanks, Mom—I'm glad, really glad. And say, Mom—you can make the **best** potato soup!"

## CHAPTER III

Jim Wilson

THE basement room was crowded, and a steady hum rose from the boys gathered into four rows of folding chairs. As Mike Spann, the scoutmaster, entered, he heard a sharp crash, as a chair went over backward and its former occupant landed on the floor with a startled yelp.

"Hello, boys." Mr. Spann was striding briskly to the front of the room. "Let's stand and give the Scout oath."

The chairs squeaked across the cement as twenty-five boys got to their feet. Hurry's chair went over backward, which was no surprise to anybody. That happened to Hurry oftener than not.

"On my honor I will do my best

To do my duty to God and my country, to obey the Scout law.

To help other people at all times.

To keep myself physically strong, mentally awake and morally fit."

"All right, boys; you may be seated now." Mr. Spann wisely contemplated the ceiling as the intricate process of fitting twenty-five Scouts into twenty-four chairs resolved itself. "You know what the scout motto is," he said, when what passed for silence had been achieved. 'Be prepared' . . . that's the aim of every Scout. We've tried to train you, here in the troop, so you'll be ready for whatever you might meet. We've given you the best First Aid instruction available, so you'd be prepared for emergencies. We've given you training in artificial respiration, and by the way, some of you have already had occasion to use it." (Tommy Martin snickered into his hand and looked furtively at Hurry. Hurry just frowned and looked at Mr. Spann more intently.)

Mr. Spann smiled. "But you know, boys, I've been doing some serious thinking recently. I've tried my best, as your scoutmaster, to prepare you for everything you'll meet in this life. But I want you to be prepared for the future too. That's what's really important, fellows . . . planning for eternity. I want you to be prepared where it really counts."

Suddenly the boys were very quiet. Hurry stopped scratching his back, and Tommy stopped making faces at Jerry and turned around to look at Mr. Spann.

"You boys know what I mean when I say we're all sinners. We all do wrong . . . I do, and all of you do." Jerry remembered his mother in the kitchen, the smell of the hot soup, and the guilty feeling inside. "Because we do wrong, we deserve to go to Hell. We'll all die some day . . . you know that. You're young, but that doesn't necessarily mean it will be a long time, either. Any of us . . . all of us . . . might meet God at any moment. But God has provided for our sins, by sending His Son to die for us. By trusting in Christ, we can have our sins removed forever—erased, as if they'd never happened."

Each boy was thinking his own thoughts, and some of them squirmed uneasily. There were things each of them would like to have erased, as Mr. Spann had said, so it would be as if they had never happened.

"I'm not preaching a sermon. You're my boys, you know, and I just want to be sure you're all going to meet me in Heaven. I wanted to let you know where I stand, and to tell you I pray for every one of you every night. I hope you'll trust Christ . . . and if ever I can help you, please come and talk to me about it."

The room was very quiet; and Jerry knew he wasn't the only one who was thinking about how wonderful Mr. Spann was, with his honest face, his cheerful grin, and his teasing ways. When you saw a fellow like that, you couldn't help but want to be like him, Jerry thought. If Mr. Spann was a Christian, then it must be the right thing to do.

Just then Mr. Spann's voice came through, cutting off Jerry's thinking. "All right, time for crafts. Hurry, I'd like to see you finish tooling that leather belt today. Let's see, Tommy, will you need help on your planter? No? That's good. I can spend some time with the three boys who are beginning plastic carving today.

"Jerry, you'll be in charge of the darkroom today, please. Get out the supplies, and carefully, Jerry. Then you can sort of schedule things, and keep the fellows out of one another's hair. . . . We have two new books on wood lore, and there are a couple of you who could spend a little time in them with profit. You, Jim and Hughie

—better stay in there and get your work done for your badges, hadn't you?"

Within five minutes every head in the building was bent over some project dear to the hearts of boys. Mr. Spann spent some time with one, helped another over a tough spot, then encouraged those who were becoming discouraged with a long-lasting job. He stopped outside the door of the darkroom, where Jerry stood.

"How's it going, Jerry?"

"All right, sir."

"Developed that roll with the flower pictures on it yet?"

"It's in the solution right now, Mr. Spann. I sure do hope they turn out good."

"I think you really got a good shot there . . . maybe we ought to enter it in the newspaper contest in the city."

Jerry's eyes shone. "D'ya . . . d'ya really think they're that good, Mr. Spann?"

"Can't tell until we see them, of course, but it ought to be fun to try. Did you check your exposure time and lens opening carefully?"

"Did it just like the book—" Jerry grinned, "I think."

Mr. Spann had a twinkle in his eye as he and Jerry shared the joke. "Yep, I know — just like the picture of old Betsy the cow you took . . . just like the book! Guess I shouldn't criticize, though, Jerry. After all, you did get one foot of Betsy in the picture!"

"I've learned a lot since then, Mr. Spann. And say, wouldn't that be something, if I . . . if I even got an honorable mention in the **Post**. Wouldn't it now!" Jerry looked at his watch. "'Scuse me, Mr. Spann. I gotta get in there and check that roll."

"Your mother would be pretty proud of you all right."

Jerry opened the door carefully so no light could enter, and disappeared through the curtains. When he came out Mr. Spann was still waiting.

"Looks O. K. so far," Jerry reported.

Mike Spann smiled, "Good! By the way, there's a new boy in town, Jerry. I hope we can get him to come to Scouts. Name's Pete Laughton, lives over by the tracks on State Road. Why don't you go by and invite him to come with you, next time?"

"I guess I could, Mr. Spann. He'd like Scouts, I bet."

"I think so . . . and I'd like for you to help him make friends and get acquainted here."

Jerry squirmed a little, polished his right shoe on the back of his left trouser leg, and thought to himself, "Who, me?" But then he looked at Mr. Spann and the affectionate blue eyes seemed to give him confidence. Out loud he said, "You really want me to, Mr. Spann?"

"I really do, Jerry. I've asked him, but one of you boys could persuade him better, I think."

Jerry thought a moment. "Well, I'll sure try. I'll do my best to get him to come to Scout meeting next week."

Mr. Spann glanced over at the plastic carving group. "Guess I'd better be getting along, Jerry. Looks like Joey needs some help over there. Bring that print over to show me when you get it ready, will you?"

"You bet I will, Mr. Spann."

Jerry was busy in the darkroom, after that, showing one of the Scouts how to keep moving his roll film in the developer, and getting the negatives ready on his own roll. As he put the first one into the printbox, there was a moment's excitement, as he again thought of the **Post's** photo contest. He fastened the best negative under the clamps and turned on the printer. He watched the clock a little nervously . . . this was one print he sure didn't want to ruin! Some fun, that would be, seeing his picture printed in the **Post,** with his name under it. **"Mr. Jerrold Thomas,"** it would say, **"of Whittenburg."** Jerry was having such a good time thinking about his name in the paper he had completely forgotten about the negative in the printbox. Suddenly his eyes focused on the second hand in horror. The timer wasn't working! He had overexposed the print!

Quickly, Jerry removed the print, and his heart sank. It was hopelessly overexposed, the picture he had hoped to submit in the contest. The background was a solid, heavy black, with no detail whatsoever. No picture for a photo contest, certainly.

Jerry whirled to the boy beside him. "Ken, what's wrong with the timer? It's not working right! My picture's ruined!"

Ken shifted uneasily. "I don't know. Jim Wilson was fooling with it a minute ago."

With an object for his resentment, Jerry's irritation suddenly became real anger. He burst out of the door of the darkroom, not even being careful about the safety

curtains that were inside the door. "Why the dirty bum! He's ruined my picture! That makes me so mad!"

Mr. Spann had heard Jerry's outburst, and started across the room toward him. The troubled look on his face made a funny feeling in Jerry. Maybe it was a little silly to get mad at Jim, after all. It would be easy as pie to make another print, and here he was making a fuss over it. He looked down at the ruined picture, which seemed a little fuzzy now.

"What's the matter, Jerry?"

"Timer's off on the printbox, Mr. Spann. Jim Wilson was fooling with it."

"'That won't be hard to fix. What's so tragic about it?"

The anger was all gone now. Jerry felt just plain foolish.

"Oh, nothing, I guess. It was my picture for the contest. I guess I got a little excited."

"Let's see it." Mike Spann looked at the damp print with interest. Jerry expected him to hand it back with disgust, but instead he kept looking at it.

"That's rather an interesting effect, Jerry, to have all the background burned out, with just the flower details showing." His eyes twinkled. "Bet you couldn't have done it if you'd tried!"

"No, sir, I guess not." Jerry looked doubtfully at the print. "Maybe I should thank Jim Wilson, instead of getting mad."

"Well, at least you should apologize. No point in getting mad, anyway, over a little thing like that. You can always make another print, you know."

"Yes, sir. That's right. Don't know why I had to go and get so silly mad."

Mr. Spann was still staring thoughtfully at the picture. "As a matter of fact, something out of the ordinary like this might be just the thing for the **Post** contest."

Mr. Spann handed the print back. As Jerry took it his mother's voice came back to him . . . "It's always easier to do wrong than right . . ." And then he could hear Mr. Spann, in Scout meeting . . . "We all do wrong . . . all of us do."

And Jerry went back into the darkroom feeling mighty uncomfortable.

## CHAPTER IV

**The Evangelist**

THE door of the Thomas home opened as if it had a gust of wind behind it, slammed with the husto of a hurricane, and Hurry Watson hurried in. His red hair looked as if it hadn't been combed for a week, and his eyes were two blue blazes.

"Hey, Jerry!"

"Hi, Hurry. What's cooking?"

"Plenty, looks like. There's a big tent going up on the vacant lot across from school, Jerry. Reckon there's a circus coming to town?"

"I hadn't heard about it. Seems like there'd have been signs or something. Wonder what's happening?"

"Mom said she'd heard something about a tent being put there, but she didn't remember what for. Tell you what, let's go down and look it over."

"O. K., Hurry. Just wait a minute till I get this rudder on." Jerry adjusted the tiny rudder on the model airplane he was making, applied glue carefully, let it dry to just the proper consistency, and then pressed the two pieces together firmly.

"There's a whole bunch of people there. Man, there's a lot of work to putting up one of those big babies."

"How many poles has it got?"

Hurry thought a moment. " 'Bout a million, I should think."

Jerry laughed. "Oh, Hurry . . . that's not the way you count tent poles. In a big tent you count the main posts —those big center poles. You know, they look like telephone poles. Usually a circus has a three-pole tent."

"Oh, I see. Well, I didn't stop to count. There were so many people around I couldn't tell anyway. Hurry up, Jerry. That glue's dry by now."

Jerry placed the plane on the shelf reserved for his collection. This one was to be a model Aeronica, and it was already looking good even though there was more work to be done on it.

"O. K. Let's go," Jerry said, wiping his hands on his trousers (a practice his mother deplored but had been unable to stop). Hurry was already out the front door by the time Jerry got there, and it was a quick trip to the vacant lot the boys cut across on their way to school.

"Never saw so many people on this lot before," Jerry said. "Say, that is a big tent. Funny they don't have any signs up."

"There's a sign over in the corner—they're starting to put it up right now," Hurry said. "Come on, Jerry — let's go over and see. Doesn't look like a circus sign, though—no pictures, anyway."

A group of men were working about a large sign, white with red and black lettering. Hurry started spelling out the words as they approached.

"E-V-A-N- . . . Evangelist James Clifton."

# REVIVAL

Jerry suddenly remembered. "Oh, yeah—they announced it in our church Sunday—I forgot."

"Whittenburg Revival Campaign," Hurry continued. "Hey, it's not a circus after all. What's Whittenburg Revival Campaign, Jerry?"

Jerry smiled over his superior knowledge. "It's like church, Hurry, only different, a little. I mean, you have a preacher, and a choir and everything, but the music's a little—oh, faster, maybe—livelier."

Hurry's mouth flew open. "Church . . . in a tent? C'mon now, Jerry, you don't expect me to believe that, do you?"

"Sure, that's what it is! They do it every year in some places. It's a special kind of church."

Just then one of the men working on the sign looked up. "Hi, boys."

"Hello," chorused Jerry and Hurry together.

"You boys don't want a job, do you?"

Jerry and Hurry looked at each other. "Why not—it's Saturday!" Hurry answered for both.

"Good! We need some boys just about your size. Mr. Lawson's over there pounding stakes for the ropes. He needs somebody to hold them."

Jerry looked around him. "Which one's Mr. Lawson?"

"See the tall fellow in the blue shirt?"

"You mean that blond man with the sledge hammer?"

"That's the one. Just go right over and volunteer your services. He'll be pleased as punch."

So Jerry and Hurry, eager to have a part in the work which looked so important, trotted over to face Mr. Lawson.

"Hello, Mr. Lawson," Hurry said. "This is Jerry Thomas and I'm Hurry Watson . . . "

Jerry butted in to explain. "Hurry's short for Hurricane, you see, although his real name is Timothy."

"Oh, I see," the man called Mr. Lawson grinned. "Well, I'm glad to know you both. Jerry and Hurry or Hurricane or Timothy, whatever I'm to call you. What can I do for you?"

"We were hoping we could do something for **you**. That man over there by the sign said you needed somebody about our size to hold stakes for you."

"I surely do. Come on, let's get started."

So that's how Jerry and Hurry first became interested in the Tent Revival in their town. They met the genial, white-haired evangelist, who looked as if he knew all about them, and they met—and immediately idolized— the curly-headed young song leader, who was called Mel. They followed him around for an hour, hoping to be allowed to help him. The men worked hard all day, brac-

ing the big tent, stringing up light wires, building a platform, and Jerry and Hurry did a little of everything. At
suppertime, they hurried home importantly, anxious to
get back.

Hurry's mother received the surprise of her life when,
immediately after supper, he washed his face and slicked
up his hair—and both his parents were literally astound-
ed when they learned it was in order to go to church!
Jerry's mother was pleased, but not surprised. A faithful
church member, she had known about the revival and
looked forward to going.

There was an air of pleasant expectancy around the
tent when Jerry and Hurry met there, just before starting time. The smell of sawdust mingled with the tang
of new canvas, and the sound of people chatting as they
arrived and greeted friends was like a subdued county-
fair sound. From the background came faint trills of a
trumpet as the personable young songleader warmed up.
Then the piano began . . . a rousing, marching Sunday
School song. One of the ushers offered Hurry and Jerry
a job giving out songbooks to newcomers. They very
happily took over the task with all the dignity they could
muster. Jerry was surprised at how many people were
coming. The tent was already half full, and more coming all the time! Mr. Hall, the druggist, was there, with
his tiny brown-eyed wife. Mr. Haines, who ran the feed
store, came with his wife and the six girls—all of them
scrubbed to shining, with pigtails twirling as they gig-
gled self-consciously. Several of the teen-age girls were
gathered about the piano, trying to learn the new song.

Suddenly, the songleader walked across the platform to the pulpit, and the undertone of talking became a silence.

"Hello there!" Mel greeted the crowd. "My, I'm glad you all came tonight! We're glad to see you—and I hope you're as glad to be here as I am. Let's start by singing a song everybody knows—number 12 in the hymn book. Let's see — does everybody have a hymn book?"

Hurry and Jerry looked at each other with wide grins. They knew their job had been done well. The only people who didn't have hymn books were those who had refused them. Most people had taken them gladly, and the boys had enjoyed it. Almost every single person held up a hymn book.

The songleader was pleased — they could see that.

"Fine! If you all have books, we should have some good singing. You'll have no excuse! Come on, now . . .

> There's a land that is fairer than day,
> And by faith we can see it afar.

Hurry and Jerry opened their books, and sang lustily through the verse. In the chorus, the young man with the trumpet soared into such a maze of trills and notes that they almost forgot to sing. My, but it was pretty! Hurry punched Jerry in the ribs . . . "Hey, Jerry, listen to that!"

"He really knows how to blow that horn, doesn't he?"

"Yeah, and when I think about wasting time practicing that old piano . . ." (Hurry didn't stop to remember that he'd wasted very little time practicing the piano, anyway.)

"Looks like a horn would be lots more fun."

"Yeah, and I bet I could learn to play it in no time, Jerry. Why, Mel could probably teach me before he leaves here."

"Sh . . . listen to what he's saying, Hurry."

The first song was over, and Mel was introducing his trumpet solo. Oh, it was wonderful—complete with scales and runs and trills. Hurry and Jerry were transfixed!

Hurry's mind was made up. "I'm gonna see if Mom will buy me a trumpet. Bet she'd be glad if I could play like that!"

A lady in front of them with a feather in her hat turned around and stared at them. Hurry stared right back, but Jerry said, "Shhhh," and tried to look as if he didn't know the boy sitting next to him. The lady with the feather turned around, thinking her job well done, but she didn't know Hurry! More than once during the service Jerry had to poke him and say, "Behave, Hurry!" or "Be quiet, won'tcha?"

There was a row of preachers on the platform, some Jerry knew and some he didn't. The song service progressed smoothly . . . another congregational hymn, a trumpet solo during the offering, a quartet from the Baptist Church. The Methodist pastor announced prayer meeting and asked everyone to help, and Mel led in a melodious chorus. After a solo by the young songleader, Pastor Johnson—who was Jerry's pastor—introduced the evangelist. "If my people, which are called by name," he read from his Bible, "shall humble themselves, and pray, and seek my face, and turn from their wicked ways; then will I hear from heaven, and will forgive their sin, and will heal their land." Hurry settled down in the seat as if he intended to sleep through this part, but Jerry noticed he always sat up straight and looked interested when the evangelist told a story. And talk about stories—he told plenty of them! They all seemed to mean something, Jerry decided. They weren't just ordinary stories, but just the same they were interesting and some were even exciting.

A few nights later Jerry and Hurry were old-timers. They sat in the same spot each night. Jerry couldn't remember when he'd enjoyed church so much — but then he hadn't been to church in a tent, not for a long time. The sermon that night seemed aimed right at them—they could understand everything. Then, toward the end, the evangelist was very serious . . . and sort of nice, too, like Mom, when she told him she loved him and that sort of thing. His voice was friendly, and kind, and as he talked about the Lord Jesus being born on earth, and living and doing good, and then dying on the cross—you just felt as if you knew Him, some way. Jerry could see that business about dying on the cross was something Hurry hadn't thought about before. Jerry knew all about it, of course, but come to think of it, he never had exactly felt so much as if he were there before. This man, the evangelist with the snowy white hair and the kind, serious face—he made you feel as if you were . . . well, as if it was your fault, sort of, that Jesus had to die. Come to think of it, Jerry decided, if you were a sinner, it **was** your fault, partly. And everybody was a sinner, of course. Mom had reminded him of that last week.

The longer Rev. James Clifton preached, the worse Jerry felt. He thought about going swimming when Mom told him not to . . . and getting mad at Jim Wilson . . . and running off with Dad's hunting knife and losing it. Jerry thought about a lot of things that night, things he thought he'd forgotten. And he felt pretty bad about the whole thing.

He was thinking so hard about it, he was hardly paying any attention to the preacher, until he heard him say, "Now, we're going to sing. As we do, I want you to remember this. Jesus died for **you** — for you, little boy . . . for you, young woman, for you, young man . . . it was for you, mothers and daddies and boys and girls. He died to save sinners — and that's just what we all are. He wants you to come to Him tonight, to trust Him and let Him come into your heart and make you His child. As we sing this song, 'Into My Heart,' will you just do what it says? Say to Him, 'Come into my heart, Lord Jesus.' If you'll do that—if you'll let Jesus come into your heart, just come right down here and take my hand. Will you do it, just now, as we sing?"

Softly the piano played a few notes . . . The songleader sang the verse of the song Jerry knew so well from Sunday School,

> Come into my heart, blessed Jesus,
> Come into my heart, I pray . . .

And then everybody joined in on the chorus.

> Into my heart, into my heart,
> Come into my heart, Lord Jesus.
> Come in today, come in to stay,
> Come into my heart, Lord Jesus.

Jerry looked at Hurry . . . but Hurry wasn't looking at him. He wasn't laughing either, as he usually was. Hurry was looking down at his shoe, his shoe which was gently kicking the back of the seat in front of him. Jerry gulped. Something inside him seemed to be saying, "Yes, I do want Jesus in my heart. I DO want to be His child . . . ," but then he thought about Hurry. What if Hurry laughed at him? What would his mother think, and the kids at school? Mom would be glad, he knew, and so would Dad. Still, . . .

A man four rows up from Jerry left his seat, with tears in his eyes, and walked up to the front. Yes, Jerry thought, but he was a grown man. They were supposed to do things in church. Boys—my goodness, you never did see boys do anything in church except maybe give out songbooks, or whisper so loud people looked at them. They were singing the chorus again,

> Into my heart . . . Come into my heart, Lord Jesus.
> Come in today, come in to stay . . .
> Come into my heart, Lord Jesus.

Jerry wanted to say it, really and truly . . . and then he remembered. The preacher had said for him to come. He said, "Mothers and daddies and boys and girls." Jerry looked at Hurry and then he thought, "Well, I don't know about you, Hurry, but I'm going to do it. I want

Jesus to come into my heart, and I'm going to ask Him to come in. I'm going to tell the preacher, too!"

And with that Jerry gave Hurry a gentle push, stepped out into the aisle and started up to shake hands with the preacher. The aisle looked mighty long, but first thing he knew he was before the dear old preacher. There was a big lump in his throat, but the one around his heart was dissolved.

"Hello, Jerry. I'm so glad you came! God bless you, boy. You know God promised to forgive all our sins, if we would just trust Jesus. Do you want to take Him, right now?"

"Yes, sir." Jerry's lips trembled, but he was determined he wasn't going to cry in front of all those people.

"I'm glad, Jerry. He'll come into your heart, right now, and make you His child—that's what He promised. And then He tells us, He'll never, never forsake us."

That was better than ever, Jerry thought, and he grinned up at the preacher. Just then he realized somebody else was reaching up to shake hands with the evangelist. It was Hurry! Hurry had followed him down the aisle, to do exactly the same thing Jerry had done. Hurry wouldn't laugh at him—he was going to trust Jesus, too!

Hurry was having more trouble, though. There was a dirty streak down one cheek, where a stubborn tear had slipped through and been hastily wiped away by Hurry's fist. Jerry felt so glad about everything he thought he might burst, any minute! He sat down on the front seat, while the preacher talked to Hurry, and then there was Mom beside him, hugging him and saying, "I'm so glad, Jerry! I've been praying you'd do this! Now our whole family are Christians . . . Isn't it wonderful?"

Jerry didn't feel he could say much; he still had to be very careful ór the wetness in his eyes **might** turn to tears. But he nodded at Mom with a grin that told her he felt exactly the same way!

After the service, Mr. Spann was the first person to speak to Hurry and Jerry.

"God bless you, boys! I'm so glad you got that settled."

Hurry and Jerry just grinned. "Now you'll have to help me get the other fellows," Mr. Spann added.

As they walked home together that night after church, the crickets chirped. Jerry felt a little self-conscious, walking with Dad and Mom and Cynthia, that way, but he felt pretty proud, too. Just as they reached the first street light, Dad turned around. He patted Jerry's shoulder and said, "I was pretty proud of you tonight, Jerry. I'm so glad you got that settled. Now we're all going to Heaven, to be together forever!"

Cynthia breathed deeply. "Gracious! Isn't it nice to be a family?"

40

Pete

JERRY didn't feel much like trying to make friends with a sixteen-year-old, but Mr. Spann wanted Pete to come to Scouts. So Jerry made his way to State Road, one afternoon, rang the doorbell, and then stood waiting on the ramshackle porch of the house where Pete Laughton lived. He was wishing he could run, when suddenly the door opened. A thin, gaunt woman stood behind the screen door, looking suspiciously at him. Since she said nothing, Jerry figured it was up to him to begin the conversation.

"Does Pete . . . Pete Laughton live here?"

"That's right." She looked him up and down, still without a shadow of welcome or friendliness. She scratched the side of her nose thoughtfully, meanwhile waiting for Jerry to continue this strange conversation he had begun.

"Is he . . . I wonder if he's home."

"Yep."

"I'd like to see him just a minute, if I could."

"He's round in back . . . go on and see him if ye want . . . ain't no one hinderin' ye."

Jerry mumbled, "Much obliged," and hurried off the porch. A big oil drum lay on its side near the house, and a few ragged chickens scratched in the thin grass. Atop the first fence pole was a batttered old black hat. In the back yard Jerry could see a weatherbeaten old Model A car, but there was not a sign of a boy called Pete Laughton. Mighty discouraging, it was, for a boy trying to do a good deed! Jerry was about to give up and go home, when something moved under the Model A, and he saw it was a foot. He walked over to the car. It was a bit embarrassing to have to talk to a foot, but that's all Jerry could see, so he figured he'd have to try it, anyway.

"Hi there." Jerry tried to make it sound friendly, but it came out awfully flat, more like a grunt than a greeting. The foot stopped moving and lay perfectly still, like a cat waiting for you to go away so it could finish its meal.

Jerry tried again. "Hello there. Are you Pete Laughton?"

Again the foot moved, this time toward Jerry. He backed off a pace or two, and waited. The foot emerged, then a skinny leg, then a pair of oily trousers, a grimy shirt, and a thatch of blond hair waving wildly.

"Yeah . . . that's me. Whatcha want?"

Jerry laughed nervously. "Oh, hi, Pete. Well, I didn't want anything exactly. Just thought I'd come over and sort of get acquainted."

"I'm busy on this car. It's one thing after another, with a car, all the time . . . "

"Yeah, well if you're busy . . . I just thought . . . "

"What's your name?"

"Jerry Thomas. Mr. Mike Spann, our scoutmaster,

wanted you and me to get acquainted. So I thought I'd come over."

"I don't go for that scout stuff much . . . Somebody's always tellin' you what to do. I like to follow my own line of interest."

"Sure . . . well, if you don't want to, that's O.K. I don't go so much for the scouting. It's just Mr. Spann . . . he's so much fun we'd rather follow his line than our own, I guess you might say."

Pete continued his labors on the decrepit car without appearing to be aware of Jerry. Jerry stood around wondering what to do, for a while, and then he became curious about what Pete was doing. None of his friends in Whittenburg knew enough about cars to put them together. Pete's blond head had disappeared under the hood of the car.

"What are you doing now, Pete?" Jerry asked.

"Now I'm checking the spark plugs. It sure takes a pile of work to keep an engine going, I'll tell you that."

"I guess so," Jerry said. "I bet it isn't easy to learn all that either, is it?"

"Naw, you have to sort of absorb it, I guess. Now me, I don't know when I learned about motors and engines . . . just seems as if I always knew. Pop says I could make a car out of any old pile of junk, though, long's it has four wheels . . . and I sort of guess he's right."

"Boy . . . I wish you could teach me an' Hurry how."

"Hurry? He that red-headed kid?"

"Yes, he's my buddy . . ."

"I guess there's lots you could learn if you just hung

43

around. I could show you . . . only this heap of mine is a mighty old car and of course I can't show you about the new things on it."

Jerry was awed. "Is she really your own car, Pete?"

Pete's pride in the car compelled him to be gruff at this point. " 'Course it's my own car. You don't think I'd be working on anybody else's, do you?"

Jerry knew Pete didn't expect an answer to that question, and he didn't make any. Instead he stared thoughtfully at Pete's quick hands, smeared with oil, but as sure and steady as a surgeon's.

"Boy — that's wonderful, Pete," Jerry breathed. "Most fellows couldn't do that, you know."

"Yeah, you're right about that," Pete said. He worked silently for a few minutes. "When did you say your scout troop meets?"

"Thursdays, four o'clock."

"Thanks, chum. I just might come over sometime. I just might."

Jerry decided that was what he'd come for, so he might as well go home now. "Good. We'll be looking for you, Pete. And really, you'll have lots of fun. You'll like Mr. Spann, I know."

"Could be. I don't take to just anybody, you know."

"I'm pretty sure you'll take to Mr. Spann. Anybody would . . . Well, I better go now."

"So long," said Pete. His head was still under the hood and the sound was muffled.

"So long, Pete. I'll look for you Thursday at Scouts. Baptist Church basement."

* * *

Sure enough, next Thursday Pete did come to Scout meeting. When Jerry came in, Pete had already arrived and had a cluster of boys around him over in the corner, talking to them. It sounded as if he was really telling them how wonderful Pete Laughton was, Jerry thought, and then he decided that wasn't very nice to think. Pete didn't even seem to notice him or acknowledge that he was there on Jerry's invitation, but Jerry decided that wasn't important, anyway. He **was** there, and that was what Mr. Spann wanted. At least Jerry had done his best. Now it was up to Mr. Spann, Jerry felt.

Jerry was curious to know which of the craft groups Pete would join. To his amazement, Pete didn't hesitate a moment before he chose the photography group.

As they walked home, Jerry and Hurry talked about Pete.

"I was sort of anxious to see which craft group Pete would choose, Hurry."

"Yeah, I was too," Hurry said, kicking a can ahead of him.

"Didn't take him long to make up his mind, did it? He headed straight for the photography group," Jerry added.

"Probably because he liked you, Jerry. After all,

you're the one who invited him to Scouts in the first place."

"Hm-h! He didn't even speak to me the whole afternoon long! Just ignored me, completely."

"Oh, well—some fellows are like that. After all, Pete isn't one of these guys with beautiful manners."

"You're right about that. Good night, why did he have to go and join the photography group? He'll probably want to enter the **Post** contest, too."

"Yep. Bet he'd really be all out to win if he entered it, too; he seems like that kind to me."

"Guess you're right about that. Oh well, I should worry about Pete entering the contest. After all, with all the readers of the **Post** as competition, why should I worry about Pete? He's just one more boy."

Next Scout meeting Mr. Spann came over to watch Jerry mount his picture.

"You know, Mr. Spann, sometimes I look at this picture, and I think it's so pretty it's sure to win the contest. And then . . . another time I look at it and it's just a big blob of black and white spots, all blurred together."

Mike Spann laughed. "I know just what you mean, Jerry."

"Right now I'm wondering if they'll take it at all! Wouldn't surprise me if they threw it out completely! It's no good, Mr. Spann."

"Oh, now Jerry — it's unusual at least — you'll have to say that."

"Thanks to Jim Wilson! You know, Mr. Spann, I've made about six different prints from that film since —

some underexposed, some just right, some overexposed, and do you know I can't get a single one that looks like **anything!**"

"Guess Jim Wilson did you a favor, didn't he, Jerry?"

"He sure did, Mr. Spann. I'm still ashamed of the way I got mad and spouted off my mouth."

"We usually get in trouble when we lose our tempers, I've found that out. And 'spouting off the mouth' seems to be the easiest way to do wrong. You know in the Bible, in the book of James, there's a whole chapter on the tongue, and the trouble it causes. 'The tongue is a fire, and a world of iniquity (or sin)' James says, 'and boasteth great things. Behold, how great a matter a little fire kindleth.' . . . Then he goes to tell how we can tame wild beasts — birds, and snakes, even, 'but the tongue can no man tame. It is an unruly evil, full of deadly poison'."

"Yes, sir. I'm surprised at some of the things **my** tongue says, I know that."

"By the way, Jerry . . . your tongue did a pretty good job on Pete Laughton, it seems. You got him to come to the meeting, didn't you?"

"Yes, sir, I guess so. He hasn't spoken to me yet . . ."

"That's just the way Pete is, I guess. You keep on and make friends with him, Jerry. Maybe you can win him to the Lord."

"Why—I—uh—I'll leave it to you to do that, Mr. Spann."

"Well, of course, we'll all work together. But there'll be some people I can't win, Jerry."

"Oh, Mr. Spann—**anybody** would listen to you!"

"Thanks, Jerry, But no, not anybody. There are some people I will be able to win—some people that won't ever find the Lord, unless I show them the way. And it's a funny thing, Jerry, but there will be some people nobody can lead to Jesus but you."

Jerry looked mighty sober about that. He'd never thought before that boys were supposed to help people find Jesus. He thought that was for preachers, and men like Mr. Spann.

"So . . . I want you to keep that in mind, Jerry. It may turn out that Pete's yours, and not mine at all."

"I don't think so, Mr. Spann. I don't think Pete likes me. But . . . I will think about it. Say, Mr. Spann, is Pete entering the **Post** contest?"

"Yes, he is. He's been trying lots of new devices, and has taken pictures of some subjects that were rather . . . different. I think he's really come up with something in his last experiment."

Jerry felt a twinge of feeling he knew must be envy, but he tried to down it and said, "Good! What's it like?"

"It's an experiment in table-top photography, Jerry. You know, that's where you take—oh, just about anything —little glass figures, fruit and vegetables or whatever you take a notion to use. You take a picture of them on a table or flat surface. Pete really has quite a clever idea."

"That's good. At least he'll keep coming to Scouts as long as he's interested in photography. He hasn't a dark-room at home."

* * *

A few minutes later Jerry stepped into the room where the developer was. There spread out on a table, was a beautiful print of—what was it, boys and girls? Jerry took another look, astonished at the quality of the print. Then he saw it was not boys and girls at all, but china figurines, with an improvised background, on the top of a table. Jerry suddenly realized that this was what Mr. Spann had called table-top photography. The next minute he realized that this was probably Pete's contest picture!

Just about the same moment, he saw a dark pool of fluid spreading from an overturned bottle, which had just reached the edge of the picture. For a moment Jerry thought, "What if Pete couldn't enter the picture in the contest?" The thought came to his mind so fast, he hardly even thought it at all. But the next minute he grabbed the picture, just before the brown stain entered the actual picture area. Already one side of the border was stained and ruined, but not the picture itself.

"Pete," Jerry called. "Hey, Pete—this your picture?"

"Sure it is," Pete said as he sauntered up, with complete unconcern. "What about it? How'd you know it was mine, anyway."

"Pete, look . . ."

Just then Pete's eyes took in the ugly brown stain at the edge of the picture. "Jerry," he yelled, "What have you done to my picture? Where'd you get it, anyway?"

"Now, wait a minute, Pete. I didn't do anything. Somebody turned over a bottle, I guess. But the picture's O.K. I picked it up and wiped it off, quick, before it got to the picture. See, it's just on the border. It's not really hurt at all."

Pete was somewhat mollified, but he still acted as if Jerry had deliberately ruined the picture. "What's the matter, Jerry—'fraid I'll win the **Post** contest?" he sneered.

Jerry's temper rose a little at that, and he started to say something. Then he remembered what Mr. Spann had said about the tongue. "What a great matter a little fire kindleth," Mr. Spann had said.

"No, Pete," he said, "I'm not worried. If your picture is best, then I want you to win. Good night, Pete!" he added hotly, "I could have let your whole picture get ruined, but I didn't. I called you instead."

Pete didn't go so far as to look ashamed of himself— that just didn't go with his manner—but he did quiet down instantly. "Yeah—that's right. Thanks, Jerry. I did want to win. That . . . $50.00 sort of meant a lot to me."

The $50.00 prize looked pretty good to Jerry, too, but he didn't say anything about that.

"Well, anyway"—Jerry grinned, "I'm sure glad I don't have to judge that contest."

"Me, too," said Mr. Spann, walking up behind Pete. "They're both good pictures and I'll just have to say, 'May the best man win'."

To Jerry's astonishment, Pete shrugged off Mr. Spann's hand, and the look he gave the scoutmaster was even worse than the way he had looked at Jerry, a few minutes earlier. Why, Jerry wondered, did Pete dislike Mr. Spann so? He could hardly believe it!

## CHAPTER VI

Mr. Thomas

JERRY and Hurry had been looking forward to Memorial Day at the County Fair ever since last year. My, what a time they had had! They had visited every exhibit, carried home a stack of literature three inches high, gotten sick on popcorn, cotton candy, and pop—and had a wonderful time. This year they expected to have even more fun, because they had prepared for it. Hurry's paper route and Jerry's lawn mowing were with a purpose—to get spending money for the County Fair.

In one of their many discussions of Memorial Day, Jerry thought of Pete Laughton.

Jerry was quiet for a moment, and Hurry looked at him. "What's eatin' you, Jerry?"

"I was just thinking about Pete, Hurry. Do you s'pose we should ask him to go to the fair with us? He might not have anybody to go with."

"Aw, I wouldn't worry about Pete, Jerry. He probably wouldn't even want to go with us, being older and all."

Jerry looked thoughtful. "Maybe not . . . but still, Mr. Spann did ask me to sort of look out for him. It wouldn't hurt to ask him to go."

"Aw, Jerry, we always have a good time by ourselves. Besides, Pete hasn't been very friendly."

"Yeah, you're right. I guess we'd better just forget it. Say, Hurry, what about riding our bikes out?"

"Might be fun. How far is it to the Fair Grounds?" Hurry was intent on a fly buzzing round his head.

"Oh, four or five miles, I guess, not too far. We've ridden that far lots of times," Jerry said.

"I'd just as soon. It's a good day for bike riding." With a sudden movement Hurry caught the fly in his hand. "There! I've got you now!"

"Yeah . . . I don't know if we'll feel that way tonight, though."

"Say, that's an idea. We're going to be mighty tired to ride home. Guess we'd better go with our folks, Jerry."

Finally, the day came—it was Memorial Day and the biggest day yet at the Fair, a real red-letter day.

Jerry sat at the kitchen table, eating puffed wheat. Mom was buttering the toast as it popped out of the toaster. Dad was reading the weekly county paper.

"Looks like a big day at the County Fair. What time do you want to leave, Lucy?"

"Guess we ought to be ready about 9:30. I want to finish making sandwiches for our lunch, and then I'll dress and be ready to go."

Jerry was so excited he could hardly swallow, but he had to finish eating so he could go and make plans to meet Hurry after they arrived at the Fair Grounds. Just as Jerry reached the last bite, he realized his dad was talking.

"Lucy, looks like there's a criminal somewhere in this vicinity!"

Jerry's eyes opened wide. He looked at his mother and she looked at his dad.

"Yep, that's right." Dad nodded his head gravely. "Herman the German, they call him."

Jerry suddenly remembered—he had seen that name before.

"Say, Dad—that's the one they have up in the post office—has a picture of him, with those other fellows, and it says 'Wanted.' He's the one with the mustache."

"It says here he escaped from prison in Canada, and they think he's headed for Chicago."

"Maybe—maybe Pop Sheehan might catch him—do you s'pose, Dad?"

Mr. Thomas smiled, more to himself than at Jerry. "Well, Jerry, Pop's a good sheriff, I guess. He does all right at jailing the drunks and tracing chicken thieves. But he's never caught a real criminal, not that I can remember."

Jerry spooned up the last of the cereal, and suddenly he had an idea. "Excuse me, Dad—I'll be back by the time Mom's ready to leave for the fair."

"All right," Mr. Thomas answered, "But be sure you . . . well, what do you know about that! He's already out the door!"

Jerry was anxious to tell Hurry all about the criminal, but when he said "Herman the German," Hurry knew all about it. "Nothin' to get excited about, though. Shucks—why do you think he might be here?"

"Listen here, Hurry Watson, you don't have to be so smart. Now just think a minute. If you were 'Herman the German,' trying to get from Canada to Chicago, and the police were after you, what would you do?"

Hurry munched his apple thoughtfully. "I don't know —what's that got to do with it, anyway?"

"I'll tell you what I'd do. If I wanted to get to Chicago, and if the police were after me, I'd settle down for a while in some little town about—well, say about fifty miles out of Chicago."

Hurry's jaw stopped moving, abruptly. "Yeah, but— that's just where Whittenburg is."

"That's what I mean, Hurry. And besides that"— Jerry's chest swelled importantly as he prepared to share his big discovery—"there's something else I bet you hadn't thought of, Mr. Smarty. You know Candy Craig's uncle is visiting them."

"Sure, I know it. Mr. Winkle, his name is."

"Yes, and I bet you didn't think of this. She says he speaks **German**."

Hurry looked at Jerry as if he'd just killed a toad. "Do you meant to tell me, Jerry, that you think Candy and the Craigs have a **criminal** visiting them?"

"Oh, I don't think that," Jerry hurried to explain, "if they KNEW he was a criminal. But what if he's just fooling them! What if he isn't Candy's uncle at all . . . maybe he's just somebody that knew him in Germany."

Hurry was visibly impressed, and yet he still was doubtful. "Seems like they'd know it if he was. I don't know, Jerry, maybe we've been reading too many of those boy detective books."

"I don't think so—I think it's perfectly possible. Wouldn't that be something to really set Whittenburg on its ear! Having a real criminal visiting the Craigs."

Hurry thought about the idea, and the more he thought the better he liked it. "Maybe we'd better tell Pop Sheehan!"

"Aw, listen, Hurry, you know how Pop Sheehan is. Dad says he's a good sheriff when it comes to catching chicken thieves and locking up drunks, but he's never been known to catch a real criminal."

Hurry was undiscouraged. "Yeah, but maybe he could, if we helped him. Boy, oh boy! Let's start investigating."

The fact that it was Memorial Day and the opening of the County Fair was far from the minds of the boys as they planned their detective activities. Hurry thought it would be most effective if they went up to Mr. Winkle —the man who said he was Candy's uncle—and said "Herman the German," loud and quick. "I bet he'd jump a mile," Hurry imagined. But Jerry wanted to be more subtle about it.

"Listen, Hurry. Let's go through our private hole in

the hedge, over to Craigs, and just look around. Maybe we'll see something suspicious, or get a clue."

Through the back gate they went, across the alley, and just as Jerry started to follow Hurry through the hedge, he dropped to the ground with a "Shhhh!" like a rattlesnake. A gutteral voice came through the hedge, in a foreign language.

"German!" whispered Hurry.

"Yeah—what do you s'pose they're saying?" Jerry replied.

"Wish I knew! Hey, listen—did I hear him say Mrs. Marshall?"

"Yeah, that much he said in English—Mrs. Marshall's elm tree! It's a secret meeting, Hurry!"

"Shhh! If you don't be quiet we can't hear anything!"

The gutteral voice continued, occasionally with an English phrase thrown in, and the boys listened intently.

The German was ending his converation, saying, "Auf wiedersehn, friend—until 10:15."

Hurry punched Jerry in the ribs so hard it was impossible for him to muffle the grunt. "That's when they're meeting, Jerry! Now we know when they're meeting—10:15. And it's under Mrs. Marshall's elm tree!"

Jerry was triumphant. "Say, who knows—maybe they're planning a bank robbery or something. This is really serious, Hurry!"

Hurry stopped a moment. "You don't suppose we ought to get Mr. Spann, do you?"

"Aw, he might think we were silly. Remember how he looked at us that day we went swimming?"

Hurry's face was red now, remembering what a jam they had gotten into. Both boys had really learned a lesson, that day. But this didn't seem exactly the same. After all, they reasoned, they weren't doing anything their parents had forbidden.

"I think it would be for the good of the town, Hurry, if we do manage to catch a criminal."

Hurry was quick to agree. "Yeah, and maybe they'll even put our pictures in the paper."

The boys skinned back through the hedge, and Jerry said, "Well, whatever we do, we'll just have to be at Mrs. Marshall's elm tree at 10:15."

Hurry became thoughtful. "Yeah, but Jerry—do you realize they might see us? It might even be dangerous!"

"Oh, don't worry about that. I have a plan." Jerry seemed very confident, and Hurry was impressed. "First, we'll have to get a ladder."

"What do you want a ladder for? There's only one tree in this whole block we can't climb without a ladder . . . say, I believe I get it now!"

"Sure—that's the tree by Mrs. Marshall's driveway— the only one we **can't** climb without a ladder. And if somebody's going to hold a conversation under a tree, where's the best place to be, if you don't want to be seen?"

"In the tree, of course. Good night, Jerry, I'll have to hand it to you. You really figured that one out."

Jerry smiled modestly. He didn't realize there were several things he hadn't figured out. For example, how he could understand a second conversation in German if he couldn't understand the first one, how he could go to the County Fair at 9:30 and be in Mrs. Marshall's elm tree at 10:15—oh, there were all sorts of things Jerry didn't figure out until later!

The boys hurried across the yard to get the ladder, and just then Hurry's mother called out the back door, "Timothy!"

Hurry made a face, as he always did when his mother called him by his proper name, but he answered, "Yes, Mom?"

"We're about to leave for the County Fair. Are you ready?"

Hurry looked at Jerry, and Jerry looked at Hurry. Hurry thought about all their plans, and he remembered all the cold, wet mornings he had gotten up to deliver papers. Jerry thought of all the miles he had trudged behind a lawn mower, all the errands he had run for a nickel or a dime. Both boys thought about cotton candy, pink lemonade and pop-corn, the electric milking machine, and the prize animals. Jerry whispered, "Maybe we could go out later."

Hurry thought quickly, before he called out to his mother, "Jerry and I—we kinda wanted to stay around for a while, Mom. Don't suppose we could hitch-hike out later, do you?"

"No, I wouldn't want you to do that, Timothy. It's not good for boys to be running around the country like that."

Hurry's forehead wrinkled, and Jerry thought hard. "Well, maybe we could . . . maybe . . ." Hurry stuttered and then stopped, because he couldn't think of anything. Then Hurry's mother came to the rescue!

"I know what we can do. Mr. and Mrs. Craig aren't leaving until 10:30. Maybe you boys could go with them."

Jerry breathed a sigh of relief. "That would be swell, Mrs. Watson, it sure would."

"Could you call Candy's mother, Mom, to see if it's all right?"

"I'm sure it will be, but I'll call her. What about you, Jerry? Shall I call your mother while I'm about it?"

"That would be great, Mrs. Watson. If you would."

Hurry's mother looked intently at the two boys. "I can't figure out what's come over you two! I declare, usually on Memorial Day you're pestering the life out of us to hurry and go to the County Fair. Well, guess I'd better call Mrs. Craig and your mother, Jerry." The screen door slammed as she went in the house.

In no time at all the arrangements were made, and Jerry and Hurry had a precious hour in which to do their detective work. Jerry remembered once that his mother had told him he'd have to think for Hurry and himself, too, and then he thought to himself, "That's when we're about to do something bad. But this isn't bad."

Quickly they hauled the ladder out of Hurry's garage, and around the corner to Mrs. Marshall's yard, where they leaned it against the tree. By this time it was almost 10:00.

"Guess our folks have gone to the County Fair, by this time," Hurry said. "I bet it's really good this year."

"Yeah," Jerry answered. "Now listen, Hurry, let's get some paper and pencils, so we can write down the evidence, if we hear anything."

The boys quickly climbed the ladder, into the branches of the big elm tree. They settled down with pencil and paper. Jerry had to explain to Hurry what was meant by "in-crim-i-nating evidence"—so Hurry would know what to listen for. Suddenly Hurry realized what Jerry meant—because he remembered they had left some incriminating evidence themselves . . . the ladder!

## CHAPTER VII

Herman the German

HURRY was speaking, and Hurry was rather excited. "We left the ladder. Now they'll know we're here! Good night, Jerry, looks like you'd have thought of that!"

Jerry was embarrassed. "What about yourself! I didn't hear **you** say anything about the ladder. What'll we do, Hurry?"

"Well, good night, it's too late to do anything, now. It's nearly 10:15 now, and that man will come any minute."

"Guess the only thing we can do is kick it down. That O.K. with you, Hurry? I mean, your dad won't mind, or anything?"

"Nope—let's get it down, and in a hurry. Won't do any good for us to BE up here if they can tell we're here!"

So in short order the ladder was removed—and not a moment too early. The next thing the boys knew, the little German man, called Mr. Winkle (and looking just like the picture of "Herman the German," only without a mustache) walked down the street with dignity. He waited under the tree, and presently was joined by another man, a stranger to the boys. "That's a suspicious character, Jerry," Hurry whispered, "Because after all, we know practically everybody in Whittenburg."

"Yeah," Jerry whispered back, "And Herman the German could have just shaved off his mustache, to disguise himself."

"And they're talking in German, too," Hurry said. "That doesn't mean any good!"

The rolling gutteral sound of German flowed steadily for a few minutes, but the boys in the tree could catch only a word now and then. Suddenly Hurry punched Jerry so hard he nearly fell out of the tree.

"Jerry, listen to that!"

"What did he say? Sounded like 'Are you ready to go?' to me," Jerry said.

"Yeah," Hurry replied, "looks like they're planning a getaway!"

The conversation below continued. Only occasionally did a word come through. Once Hurry thought he heard Mr. Winkle say, "row-boat," but he wasn't sure. And then, while the boys' eyes bulged, Mr. Winkle brought out a fat billfold. My, it was stuffed with bills! Hurry and Jerry looked at each other. They were sure now! This man was probably a bank-robber.

"How're we gonna capture him, Jerry?" Hurry said.

"I don't know, Hurry. We'd better wait until we're sure, anyway."

"I could break off a branch and throw it down on him. I bet that would knock him out, Jerry."

"Yeah, but . . . what if it **isn't** Herman the German? He'd be mighty mad!"

"It **must** be." Hurry insisted. "After all, we've got enough evidence now . . . "

Jerry looked worried. "Maybe we should have called

Pop Sheehan after all.  I don't know what to do."

The fat little German man lapsed into English: "Just this one day, and then I must be on my way," he said with a merry twinkle.

The other German man replied: "It has been good to see you again, friend.  And to think we have not met since the days in the Old Country."

"Is he helping him escape?" Jerry said, with a puzzled frown.

Just then, in that thick funny accent, Mr. Winkle said, "Yes, we'll have a good day today at the County Fair." Jerry and Hurry looked at one another, eyes open wide, as their so-called "criminal" continued, "And then it's back to the general store business in Bloomingdale, for me."

Jerry and Hurry exchanged anguished looks.  Was it possible that the man they had thought was a criminal was only the proprietor of a country store?  Jerry looked at the pencil he was holding so tightly, ready to take down "incriminating evidence," and Hurry muttered, "General store business!  Good night, there's nothing suspicious about that."

Jerry suddenly sat up straight, and put his pencil down. "Hurry, do you know what?  Those men were going to meet at 10:15, and the Craigs were leaving for the Fair at 10:30.  We were to meet them then.  It must be after 10:30 now and—" Jerry's voice became a wail, "Oh, Hurry—look at us!  We've kicked the ladder down!"

Hurry looked down the base of the tree, at the ground so far away, and he gulped.  "What a couple of dopes!"

But Hurry's optimistic nature was not long to be worried over the lack of a ladder. "Oh, well—why worry over a ladder. Sometimes it takes a ladder to get up a tree, but anybody with any sense at all ought to be able to shinny down a tree."

"Yeah, I guess so." Jerry was still a little doubtful. "Shall . . . shall I go first?"

"Naw, I'm down the lowest. I'll go first. You have to watch this place . . . it's tricky. You could get an arm or leg caught awful easy in a narrow crotch like this."

With much grunting, Hurry proceeded down to the lowest branch. That was the tricky one, with a narrow crotch. Jerry knew how it felt to get caught in a tree branch, from his experience in the pear-tree in his back yard. Once he'd been there half an hour before Dad had heard him hollering and had pulled him out.

"Now . . . if I can just get around to this side—it's a little smoother," Hurry was saying, and suddenly, "Ouch!"

"What's wrong, Hurry? You didn't hurt yourself, did you?"

"Well, good night!" (If you judged by Hurry's conversation, you'd get the impression it was perpetual nightfall!) "If I didn't go and" . . . each word was punctuated by a grunt . . . "get stuck!"

"Let's see," Jerry said. "Maybe I can help you." For the next few minutes the boys worked frantically. But it was no good; Hurry was stuck fast. In the tree they couldn't get enough room to really pull. "Well, I guess

I'll have to go down and get the ladder, Hurry. Maybe I can help you get out then."

"You can't get around me, Jerry. We're stuck, that's all there is to it!"

"You mean—you mean we're going to have to spend the day up here in this tree?" Jerry said.

"Well, can you think of something?"

Helplessly, the boys looked at one another, hoping somebody would have an idea. But Jerry shrugged his shoulders, and Hurry didn't have an idea, and there wasn't anybody else there to have one.

Jerry took out his $1.43, without speaking, and counted it. It was the money he had earned to spend at the County Fair . . . but now it seemed he would spend Memorial Day in a tree! Hurry took out his $2.29, and counted it. But after all, you can't just count money all day, even if you have $2.29!

"How's your leg, Hurry? Does it hurt?" Jerry asked.

"Nope; getting a little numb, but that's all. Doesn't hurt," Hurry replied. And so they sat there . . . Hurry on the bottom limb, Jerry on the second limb from the bottom, north side, of Mrs. Marshall's elm tree. They talked about the ferris wheel, they talked about the "cotton candy" booth, they talked about the cattle and the exhibits and all the literature they could be collecting —and they sat in the elm tree.

They couldn't tell what time it was, but how slowly the time crept along! Surely somebody would come by, they thought—but nobody did. It seemed fairly certain

that nobody was going to. On Memorial Day, Whittenburg was a deserted city. Their chances of getting down from the tree before evening were mighty slim.

Hurry couldn't move his leg, but his brain was busy. He kept trying to figure out a way. "Jerry, listen. Maybe our folks will miss us and come back."

Jerry's face brightened with hope for a moment—but just a moment was all it lasted. "Nope," he said with discouragement. "They'll just think we came with somebody else. You know we never see our folks at the County

Fair, except at lunch time. They'll just think we forgot to come for lunch. They won't look for us until time to come home."

Just as it seemed the boys couldn't stand it another hour in the tree, they heard footsteps. Footsteps! It sounded so loud, in the silent street, the boys almost jumped. My, but the sound of walking sounded good! "Good as firecrackers," Hurry thought, "on the Fourth of July!"

"Who is it, Hurry?" Jerry asked. Hurry was craning so far out of the tree it seemed any moment he'd be hanging by his feet.

"Can't tell. It's not any of our folks . . . it's a boy. Jerry!"

Hurry sat up so quickly he nearly knocked Jerry off his limb. "Jerry, I do believe it's Pete!"

"Pete—but what would he be doing here? Everybody's at the County Fair!"

"I don't know, but here he comes. We'll holler when he gets a little closer. He can put the ladder back up, and then you guys can help me get my foot loose."

"Hurry," Jerry looked thoughtful, "We really should have asked Pete to go with us to the County Fair. I bet he'd have gone, if we'd asked him."

"I dunno, but I'm not going to worry about that. I just hope we can get there ourselves!" Hurry was shouting now. "Pete! Hey, Pete!"

Jerry got so excited he was yelling, too. Pete looked up through the branches, astonishment on his face. "Well, for goodness' sake! What you fellows doing up there? How did you get there?"

"We used a ladder," Hurry explained breathlessly, "But after we got here, it . . . it . . . toppled over."

"We . . . pushed it a little, I guess," Jerry admitted.

"And then I started to shinny down and got my leg caught . . ."

Pete was putting the ladder back up, and in another moment, with all of them pushing and hauling, they had freed Hurry's leg.

"I was sort of looking for you guys . . . wondered if you'd like to go out to the Fair Grounds with me in the flivver."

"Would we! We'd love to," Hurry breathed.

Jerry was having a hard time with his conscience. Why in the world hadn't they invited Pete to go to the County Fair with them? After he'd promised Mr. Spann he'd try to encourage Pete, he hadn't done much about it.

Hurry ran to put the ladder in the garage, and off they went.

They got to the Fair in time for lunch, and after four sandwiches apiece, with pop, the morning spent in Mrs. Marshall's elm tree didn't seem too bad. It was a wonderful Memorial Day — and Hurry and Jerry decided later that introducing Pete Laughton to the Whittenburg County Fair had been half the fun.

* * *

That night when Jerry got home, he flopped on the porch swing. His eyes were half closed as he thought over the day.

Suddenly he sat up straight and stopped swinging. "Jerry!" his father was calling.

"What is it, Dad?" Jerry slammed the door as he ran in the house.

Dad was holding the **Post** in his hands, looking at an article at the bottom of page two. "Hey, Jerry, you remember we were talking about Herman the German at breakfast this morning? Well, here's an article in the **Post** from San Antonio, Texas. Listen to this: 'Today an escaped convict, known as Herman the German, was captured in a hotel room here with a gun he had just bought in a pawn shop. The man, who escaped from a Canadian prison last week, rowed across the Detroit River, stopped off in Chicago, and then came here. He evidently intended to get into South America through Mexico, hoping to obtain passage from there on a Germanbound ship.'"

Jerry felt pretty foolish at that. What a bright idea he had had! Thinking a poor old inocent man—from a country store nearby, and an uncle of one of his best friends—was a criminal! And what a smart detective—climbing a tree and being stuck up there half the day! All he had done, with his smartness, was miss half of Memorial Day at the County Fair.

And then he thought about Pete, and the sort of hopeful way he had asked Hurry and Jerry to go to the Fair with him. "Maybe Pete wasn't so bad after all," Jerry said to himself. "I'm going to have to try harder to be friendly with Pete. He does need the Lord Jesus for a friend."

## CHAPTER VIII

Hurry

HURRY and Jerry were fishing. That is, they were holding fishing poles before them, complete with line and bait. But apparently nobody had told the fish about it, and they weren't cooperating very well! This didn't bother Jerry and Hurry, though. It was good enough just to be sitting on the grassy bank, with the hot sun pouring down on them and the summery sounds floating all around them.

"Jerry, I just can't figure out that Pete Laughton," Hurry said.

"What do you mean, Hurry?"

"You know, Jerry. The way he is about Mr. Spann. He's the first person I ever knew who didn't like Mr. Spann."

"Yeah," Jerry answered, "it bothers me, too; seems so funny. Mr. Spann's always been nice as pie to Pete. But I guess everybody can't like Mr. Spann as well as we do." He broke off abruptly. "Hurry, sit still, for goodness' sake. How in the world can you expect to get a bite when you wiggle around all the time, and drop clods of dirt in the water, and keep stirring things up!"

Hurry grunted. "Just trying to get a little more comfortable. Hey, don't you think it's about time to eat our sandwiches?"

"Reckon it is, at that," Jerry said. "Doesn't look like we're going to get any fish, anyway."

The sandwiches were good, and with chewing to be done, there was no conversation for a few minutes. But both boys continued to think about the strange, belligerent character of Pete Laughton.

"I . . . sort of wish Pete weren't coming on the overnight hike, Hurry."

"I do too—the old sourpuss! Why does he have to go and be such a wet-blanket? Looks like if he's so dead-set against Mr. Spann he wouldn't **want** to go."

Jerry's conscience began to make itself known then. "I guess we shouldn't feel that way, Hurry. After all, we're supposed to be helping Mr. Spann lead him to Jesus."

"Oh, well," Hurry began to look on the bright side, "We'll have a good time on the overnight hike. We always do."

"Sure, Mr. Spann will see to that."

"Well, we'd better, that's all I've got to say," said Hurry, with a trace of feeling. "If Pete Laughton ruins our overnight hike, I'll . . . why I'll be so mad, Jerry, there's no telling what I'd do."

Jerry laughed. "Don't worry, Hurry. Mr. Spann knows how to plan an overnight hike, and Pete's bound to enjoy it."

"Hey, Jerry—I've got a bite. Look out!"

And with much splashing and grunting, Hurry proceeded to land a four-inch perch.

\* \* \*

72

It was Friday afternoon that the boys all met for the overnight hike. What a group that was, in front of the church! Some had on boots, some had on sneakers—there was even one barefoot boy—and their costumes were as varied as their footgear. But they had all brought along their enthusiasm and high spirits and it promised to be the best overnight hike the Whittenburg Scouts had ever had. At 4:00 Mr. Spann called the roll. Everybody was there except Hughie Mason, who had come down with measles the day before. Everybody carried some article necessary to making overnight camp—hunting knives and frying pans and flashlights and axes. What a party it was!

Up the Meadow Road they went, toward Bumpas Ridge. Up front they were clustered close together, around the scoutmaster, but in back they began to string out a bit. Every so often Mr. Spann had to call out, "Step up, everybody," so the stragglers didn't fall too far behind. Somebody started a song, and everybody joined in, tramping down hard to the rhythm of HUP-two-THREE-four. Jerry was walking with Pete, and he could hear Hurry's off-key tune up ahead of him.

"We always have a good time on the overnight hike, Pete," Jerry said, having made up his mind to be as friendly to Pete as he could be.

"Yeah, I guess. This is old stuff to me, though," Pete bragged. "I could really have more fun by myself, I guess, instead of going with a bunch of kids."

Jerry's pride was hurt, but he couldn't blame Pete for feeling that way. After all, he was several years older than the rest of the boys, and had his own car, and all.

"Well, with Mr. Spann . . ." Jerry saw the contemptuous look on Pete's face, and he stopped . . . "it's always fun," he finished lamely.

"Yeah, he's all right for you fellows. After all, you haven't been around much. I'm not used to having somebody go along to show me what to do, when I hike. Why, I went up into the Olympics once, Jerry, just me and another boy! What a time we had! We got stuck on a ridge up there—no path and no room to walk, and no handholds. All we could do was just scrape along, grabbing a few blades of grass here and a rock there."

"Say, did you, Pete?"

"Sure did. And it was getting dark, too, and we didn't have any water. Boy, I wasn't sure we'd get out of there alive! But we did; wasn't bad at all, once we got over on the other side of the ridge."

"What're the Olympics like, Pete?"

"Oh, just like the pictures. You know, they have these little lakes and little scrubby firs and spruce . . . and then after you get up a ways, no trees at all, and big stretches of ice with cracks—crevasses, they're called."

Jerry nodded knowingly. "That's what they call the timber line—where the trees stop."

"Yeah. Pretty nice. Not anything like it is out here, of course. What you call a mountain out here we'd call a foothill!"

"Guess so. But the Ridge—there are some pretty wild places up there."

"Oh, I don't know," Pete said loftily. "After all, there's no place up there where you could really get **lost**. Any

place on Bumpas Ridge is just a few hours' hike from Whittenburg, actually."

Jerry had to agree, for it was certainly true. "Still, there's lots of rugged land up there—and snakes—you should hear the snake stories they tell! Timber rattlers, they say."

"And half of them probably not true! No, I don't think I'd be scared of anything we'll find on Bumpas Ridge, Jerry."

Hurry came back to find Jerry, then. Hurry had his bird book along—he was working on his merit badge in bird study. "I saw a scarlet tanager up there, and another one I haven't found yet, Jerry. It's familiar—I know I've seen the picture. It's black all over, with a big patch of red on the wing, outlined in white."

"Yellow you mean," Pete put in. "I've seen 'em, too. That's a red-winged blackbird, isn't it?"

Hurry shook his head. "Not with that white streak, or yellow streak, or whatever you call it. The red-winged blackbird is just black with red wings, period."

"I'll be glad when you get your badge, Hurry. You're about the last one to get it in bird study, aren't you?"

"Aw, just 'cause I can't sit still and look at birds," Hurry grunted. He leafed through the book. "Hey, here it is! Look, Jerry, it's the tri-colored blackbird!"

Jerry nodded. "Yeah—pretty! Say, Pete, I see you've got your camera case. Do you think you'll get some good pictures?"

"I might. Thought I'd better be prepared."

Jerry grinned. "Nothing like the Olympics, I bet. Nothing like that out here."

Pete ignored the teasing in Jerry's voice. "A good picture's where you find it, Jerry. Now you might get a good picture right in your back yard, or just anywhere. You just have to be ready to take pictures when things happen."

"Sure, that's right," Hurry agreed.

"That's the way the news photographers do it. One day they're just walking along and—bingo, something happens. A fire, or an accident, or earthquake. They have their cameras ready, so they get a good picture. It's as simple as that."

"I guess so," Jerry said. "Except usually when fires or

floods happen, photographers don't happen to be standing there."

"The way to get good pictures," Pete affirmed (sounding like a teacher in school, Hurry thought), "is just to be prepared for them."

The sun was low in the sky when the troop reached the Scout camp on Bumpas Ridge. Mr. Spann had been up that morning in the pick-up truck, bringing the grub, and there was plenty of wood around, just waiting to be cut and stacked. Quickly the scoutmaster assigned the jobs; five or six to cutting boughs for the beds, others to cutting wood for fire, two or three to build the fire they would cook on. Some he set to cleaning out the cabin, and to Jerry and Hurry he gave the job of getting water from the spring.

"That Pete and his stories about the Olympics!" Hurry snorted. "Why didn't he stay there?"

"I think it's sort of interesting, Hurry. He doesn't mean to be bragging. It's just his way."

"Huh! Well, I'm not crazy about his way."

When they got back to camp, the hot dogs were steaming and the place was beginning to look shipshape.

By 7:30 or 8:00 the meal was eaten, and there were some good, fast games; Steal the Bacon, Prisoner's Base, and Kick the Can—all old favorites. Then the bedrolls were laid out as each fellow staked his "claim", and the boys dropped down around the dying fire. All the old camp songs they sang, one after another. "I've Been Workin' On the Railroad," "Row, Row, Row Your Boat," "Scotland's Burning," "Bill Grogan's Goat," and "Casey Jones." During a lull between songs, Mr. Spann stood up.

"Sounds good, fellows, mighty good. It's great to be with a group of boys like you. I'm fond of every single one of you, and I hope Scouts can mean to you what it has meant to me. We've got a night and a full day ahead of us before we start home tomorrow night. There are a few things I'd like to say to you as we begin this time together. First of all, I want you to have a good time. If we all work together, we can make it the best overnight hike there's ever been. I'm planning on that, and I know it's what you want, too. Second, there's one essential I'd like to emphasize. When there are this many people out in the rough, a lot of things can happen. There is just one way for us all to be safe and happy, and that is to obey rules. The rules aren't made to keep you from having a good time . . . They're made so we can all have a good time. If we all obey the rules, we won't have anything to be sorry for when we head for home tomorrow night."

A big log broke in two, and in the flare of light Jerry noticed Pete, across the circle from him. There was a hard look on his face that worried Jerry. Why, Jerry wondered, does Pete resent everything Mr. Spann says?

"And the third thing—it's the most important of all. You fellows know that the Lord Jesus Christ is the most important Person in my life. He's saved me from my sin, and I love Him more than anything in the world. Many of you know what I mean, because you're Christians too." (When Jerry heard Mr. Spann talk like that, he was mighty glad he'd lined up on the right side during the revival!)

"One of my biggest thrills came when I saw Hurry and Jerry go down the aisle one night to trust Christ, and the next night five or six other fellows did the same thing. I'm glad that most of you have done that. But there are still a few who haven't done it. I won't embarrass you—you know in your heart whether or not you've settled this thing. But listen, fellows. I'm praying that not one of you will go home from this overnight hike away from the Lord. Let's all be on the same side. You who haven't trusted Christ, won't you do it now?"

The circle was absolutely quiet. All the giggling and pushing had stopped. Every boy was looking straight at Mike Spann, as he spoke from his heart.

"Here's a fagot I'm holding in my hand. It's burning, and I'm going to let it represent my life and heart. Each one of you, will you take a stick, and light it?"

In a moment of scrambling, every boy had his fagot lighted, and they sat back expectantly for Spann's next word.

"Now—here's my fagot. As I said, I'm going to let it represent my life. We'll let the campfire represent God and His plan for us. Already I've said in my heart, 'God, you can have me. I'll trust you as my Lord and Saviour, and I want to be what you'd have me to be.' I still feel that way tonight, boys, and as a sign of that I'm going to throw my fagot—my life—into the fire. I'm giving myself anew to Christ, who's already saved me."

The fagot made a wide arc, and landed in the middle of the dying fire with a shatter of sparks.

"You who've already done it—who've trusted Christ—

will you join me in it? Just toss your fagot in, too, as a sign that you've given yourself to God."

From every side of the circle, the fagots curved easily into the fire. It blazed up with new flame, lighting the serious faces around the circle. Jerry felt a deep peace within him as the rough stick left his hand and fell into the fire.

"Some of you still have your fagots," Mr. Spann continued. "That means, I take it, that you haven't yet taken the step I'm talking about. I'd like to remind you that Jesus Christ died on the cross for you—and He wants you to trust Him. You ought to do it, boys. Will you, right now, say in your heart, 'Lord Jesus, I'll take you.' If you will, fling your fagot in with the rest."

Only four flames were left around the circle. Every boy seemed to hold his breath as one wavered, and then arched into the fire. Another (held by Jim Wilson, Jerry could see in the flickering light) was tossed lightly into the fire. The third one landed almost at the same time. Only one flare left! And above it Jerry could see Pete Laughton's face — hard, defiant, angry.

"Throw it, Pete," Jerry was saying to himself. He wanted Pete to do it so badly he could almost do it for him. "Please, Pete! Do it!" he thought.

Suddenly, Pete Laughton whirled. Swiftly, he threw his fagot—away from the fire, far, far out into the woods, as far as he could throw it!

There was a stunned silence. Then Pete began running, toward the spot where the fagot had landed, away from the campfire circle.

## CHAPTER IX

**Mike Spann**

MIKE Spann's heart ached for Pete, out alone in the woods, but he knew the boy would have to fight it out alone. There was a tense silence over the circle of boys, and Mr. Spann spoke quietly.

"I'm so glad you fellows decided that way—Tommy, Jim, and Dave. It's great to be the sons of God—and that's what He makes us when we trust Him. Now remember, we can depend on Jesus for everything we need. When you trust Him, He forgives your sins, and you become His child."

Mr. Spann prayed then, asking God to give them a good weekend. And at the end he said, "And bless Pete Laughton. Be with him, and help him to find Thee this weekend." When Mr. Spann said Amen, there was an unspoken echo in the heart of every boy in the circle.

Hurry was the first one awake, the next morning. He woke up Jerry, and the first thing they did was look at Pete's bedroll. He was there, sound asleep. Just by tiptoeing around and whispering (in Hurry's own manner) Hurry soon had the whole camp awake, and ten minutes later it was a beehive of activity. The bacon smelled wonderful, and there were twenty-five Scouts who thought it was great to be alive, that morning on Bumpas Ridge.

After breakfast there were clean-up chores to be done, but before very long the camp was in apple-pie order, the Scouts were ready for a day's outdoor activities.

Mr. Spann called the group together. "All right, boys. We'll spend the rest of the morning on our hike over to the Knob. First of all, I want to remind you to keep your eyes open. One of the most important things for a Scout to learn is to observe. Notice what's going on around you. Watch out for unusual plants (and that includes poison ivy!) Look for birds you haven't seen before. Watch where the rest of us are—we don't want anybody lost on this trip! And finally, look out for danger. That may be in the form of a sudden break in the trail . . . a slippery spot along the cliff, a spider in a rotten log, or you may even see a snake coiled on a sunny rock. I don't have to tell you to consider every snake a poisonous one until you know differently, and most important of all, **don't take any chances!**"

There was a pleasant scurry of activity as the boys strapped on their knapsacks and started down the trail. Hurry struck up his favorite song, "There's a Long Long Trail A-Winding" (**why** it was his favorite, nobody knew; he never spent any time dreaming that any of the boys had ever seen) in a loud, off-key wail, and others joined him. At first the boys traveled in a tight group, but gradually they began to string out in smaller bunches. Jerry and Hurry found themselves a little ahead of the rest, with Pete Laughton and Jim Wilson. Pete thought the idea of finding any danger on Bumpas Ridge was ridiculous, but he adjusted his camera thoughtfully, obviously expecting to get a good roll of negatives. His old bravado was back, with the slightly contemptuous manner he used in talking to the younger boys. Jerry remembered last night at the campfire, and he felt a little sorry for Pete.

"Yep," Pete was saying, in his superior voice, "ought to get some great old pictures today. You fellows tell me, now, if you see anything that would make a good picture."

Hurry was watching for birds, and Jerry was just enjoying the outdoors, and so before they realized it, the four boys were far ahead of the others.

"Hey, I can't even hear the rest of the fellows," Jim Wilson said.

"Oh, that's all right. We don't have to stick right with them," Pete assured him.

"Yeah," Hurry put in, "But Mr. Spann said . . ."

"I'm tired of what Mr. Spann said!" Pete said, angrily. "If you don't mind, just leave him out of this. I know enough about the woods I don't have to keep talking about what Mr. Spann said."

Jerry felt mighty uncomfortable, and Hurry threw Pete a puzzled look. Jerry finally decided there was nothing to do except try to get back with the group as soon as they could. He didn't like the way Pete was acting, though, and he felt as if he couldn't trust him.

Jim Wilson stopped suddenly. "What was that moving, just then?"

All the boys stopped.

"Where, Jim?"

"Right there—through the trees, on that rock."

Pete had brushed past Jim and the other boys. "It's a snake! Hey, you guys, I bet I can get a swell picture here!"

"Pete, stop! Don't get so close," Jerry called.

"Aw, don't be such a baby, Jerry. Look, he's perfectly quiet." Pete was fiddling with the aperture adjustment on his camera, squinting through it, getting ready for a picture.

"Boy—what a picture!" Hurry said. "Good boy, Pete!"

Pete took one picture, and moved around to another angle to take two more.

"C'mon, Pete," Jerry said. "You know what Mr. Spann . . . you know we are s'posed to be careful of danger—and that snake could be awful dangerous."

Pete glared at Jerry. "All right, Mr. Smarty. What would you say if I told you this isn't even a poisonous snake. It's perfectly harmless."

"What makes you think so, Pete?"

"I can tell. After all, I know a few things," he said belligerently.

"I don't think so, Pete," Hurry put in. "I think it's a timber rattler."

Jerry could hear the voices of some of the other boys, approaching down the trail.

"Well, Mr. Spann will be here in just a few minutes. Why don't we just wait and let him see it."

"O.K., O.K.," Pete said. "He can see it if he wants to. I don't care if he looks at it all day. But I'm going to get an action picture, if I can." Pete picked up a stone.

"You're not gonna throw it, are you, Pete?" Hurry said anxiously.

"Sure I am. Why not? I get so sick and tired of you fellows trying to tell me what to do!"

"But Pete . . ."

The rock whizzed out of Pete's hand, struck the rock, but missed the snake.

Jerry could see that the more they said, the madder and more reckless Pete got. If only Mr. Spann would hurry! Jerry suddenly decided maybe the best thing to do would be to go back and get the scoutmaster. Without saying anything, he slipped away, back down the trail, toward the group, running as fast, and as quietly, as he could.

Pete was so intent on the snake he didn't even notice that Jerry was gone, and Hurry and Jim—well, they were just plain scared. They knew what had happened to Kenny Small, when he had gotten bitten by a rattle snake on this very ridge, and they weren't happy about Pete's tantalizing this snake, even if, as he said, it was a harmless one. They couldn't see too well, but it **did** seem to have rattles.

Pete stooped over—as if he had all the time in the world—and chose another stone. This time, he took aim, and the stone went one—two inches or so from the snake's head.

The evil eyes were fixed, it seemed on Pete.

Pete's excitment was growing. "Say, wouldn't it be something if I could get him roused up, and **then** get a picture? That would really be a prize-winner." Pete was reckless by nature, and now he was so carried away with the idea he lost all thought of danger. He grabbed a short stick, walked right up to the snake, and prodded it.

Hurry gasped. "Pete, please don't."

"Listen, Hurry, stop worrying. Nobody's going to get hurt. Besides, if this snake did strike, I could move quick enough."

"No, you couldn't! They move quick as lightning, when they strike."

Again, Pete prodded the snake with his stick. The head lifted warily, and the wriggling body became a coil.

"There now," Pete said, "if I can just get a picture."

"That snake's about to strike, Pete." Jim shouted.

"I'll just get a picture," Pete said breathlessly. Pete was beginning to realize the danger now, but Hurry knew he was determined to get a picture before the snake moved.

He was very close to the rock, within a few feet of the coiled reptile. Pete's fingers shook as he adjusted the camera, fumbling. The snake's head drew back slowly, prepared to strike.

"Pete!" Hurry was screaming now. "Pete, move!"

The next few minutes were a blur to Hurry. He heard running feet behind him on the trail, but he couldn't take his eyes from the snake, moving quickly and surely now, and from Pete, crouched by the rock, frozen. Suddenly the movement came—what Hurry had known all along was going to happen. The snake struck out cruelly toward Pete's bare arm, holding the camera. At that instant—Hurry would never know how it could happen— a heavy leather boot was thrust before the snake's head. There was a soft thud, as the fangs struck in the leather, struck and held. It was Mr. Spann! He had taken the bite —had saved Pete's life!

Pete, white and shaken, had sat down abruptly on the ground, his camera forgotten. Scouts were running up. Hurry was weak with relief. Pete hadn't been hurt! He had made the snake strike, but he hadn't been bitten. Then, Hurry realized that Mike Spann was on the ground, and Jerry was bending over him. He ran over.

"Jerry, he's not hurt, is he?"

"Mr. Spann, what's the matter? Did he get through the boot?" Jerry was asking, anxiously.

"Let's get the boot off and see, Jerry. Unlace it, will you? The boot's thick enough, I knew that. But looks like one fang went in at the edge of the lacing, through the tongue."

The snake slithered off the rock and away into the woods.

Quickly, Jerry unlaced the boot, turned down the heavy sock. There it was, a tiny prick. No bigger than a pin would make!

"Yes, guess he got me, Jerry. Well, better call Tommy. He has the First Aid kit and the snake kit. This won't be a very nice business, I'm afraid."

Tommy had rushed up, and in another second the snake kit was open on the ground.

Jerry thought rapidly. "Listen, guys, you better fix up some kind of stretcher we can carry Mr. Spann back on, while we're doing what has to be done here."

Pete looked white still, almost sick, but he knew how to make a litter and he took charge of the project immediately. Soon he had four or five scouts working and the stretcher began to take shape. None of them could really concentrate on their work, though. Their eyes were drawn, again and again, to the spot where Mr. Spann sat on the ground, cutting an "X" in the flesh over the pinprick. They watched Jerry then as he drew the poison from the wound with the suction cup, put in antiseptic, and then bandaged it. Feverishly the boys worked, tying the vines into place to make a solid framework on the stretcher.

It was placed on the ground beside Mike Spann, and gently he was lifted on. It was a sober group of boys that started back down the ridge they had climbed so happily a few minutes earlier.

## CHAPTER X

THE long, long hike back to town would stand out in his mind forever, Jerry thought. He knew they had done all they could for the snakebite. He had acted as quickly as possible and Mr. Spann had given him instructions, but still Jerry knew it was serious. People usually died if they were bitten by a poisonous snake, he knew that.

"Mr. Spann . . ." Mr. Spann's eyes opened, looking very blue in his white face. "That was a timber rattler, wasn't it?"

"Yes, Jerry."

"And they **are** poisonous, aren't they?"

"I'm afraid so—very much so."

"Will . . . will you be all right, Mr. Spann?"

"You won't . . . die, will you, Mr. Spann?" Hurry said.

Jerry kicked Hurry. "What a thing to say!" he whispered fiercely.

"I don't know, Hurry. If I should die, why, I'm ready to go to Heaven. But they may be able to do something at the hospital. It's in the Lord's hands, anyway."

"There's the Moore's farmhouse, Mr. Spann," Jerry said. "I'm going to run ahead and phone for an ambulance. You fellows don't jog him any more than you have to, now!"

And so the Scout overnight hike for that year ended

with Mr. Spann in the hospital with a poisonous snake bite. Hurry and Jerry remembered the day they had sat on the bank fishing, when Hurry had said he hoped Pete didn't ruin the overnight hike. It seemed Pete had done just that. Still, they had had that wonderful time around the campfire, and Tommy and Jimmy and Dave had made their decisions for Christ.

The doctors worked hard on Mr. Spann. The first time Mr. Spann could see visitors, Jerry went to see him. As he sat in the waiting room of the hospital, Dr. Lewis came striding through.

"Dr. Lewis," Jerry called, "How's Mr. Spann getting along?"

"As well as can be expected, Jerry. No, actually much better than that. He was in great physical condition, you know, and that helped."

"Oh, yes, sir. Mr. Spann always has been so healthy."

"Yes, and then he got good, prompt care. It's just a

good thing he was with a bunch of Scouts. Jerry, or we might not have saved him. Even with that, it was rough going those first two days."

"He . . . did he nearly die, Dr. Lewis?"

"He came very, very close to it, Jerry."

"If it had been somebody . . . somebody that didn't have on a boot, and got the full force of the bite—they probably wouldn't have lived, would they?"

"No. I guess that leather boot did save his life. He got a lot of poison as it was, but only one fang actually pierced his skin."

"And he . . . Mr. Spann saved somebody else's life, Dr. Lewis, when he put his foot out."

"I should think so, Jerry, if he came between the snake and somebody it was striking at; yes, I should say he saved their life." The doctor looked at his watch. "Guess I'd better check Room 30 now. So long, Jerry."

Jerry sat down again to wait for the nurse who was going to take him to Mr. Spann. Just then he noticed that someone else had come in during the conversation with the doctor. Pete Laughton was sitting across the room!

"Hi, Pete."

"Hello, Jerry." Pete looked acutely embarrassed . . . and Jerry realized it was the first time he had seen Pete without his look of arrogance.

"You going to see the scoutmaster, Jerry?" Pete asked.

"Soon's the nurse comes back and says I can. You goin' in too, Pete?"

"Nnnn-nope. I'd feel too funny t..t' talk to him. I just

wondered if you'd tell him . . . (there was more than a suspicion of a tear in Pete's eye) . . . that I sure do appreciate what he did for me."

"O.K. But . . . he'd want you to come in yourself, Pete."

Pete gulped. "When a fella saves your life . . . well, that's really something. And when he gives up his own—when he really takes a chance on dyin' himself—when he doesn't owe you anything—well, there's not much you can say about that."

Suddenly Jerry thought about what Mr. Spann had said. "There will be somebody nobody can lead to Jesus but you," Mr. Spann had said. "It may turn out that Pete's yours, and not mine at all." Jerry's eyes were shining as he turned to Pete.

"But don't you see, Pete, that's just the way it is with the Lord Jesus! That's just what He did—give up His own life for you! He died on the cross for you—for me—for all of us, to save us. That's why He wants you to trust Him, to accept Him into your heart."

Pete frowned slightly, thinking hard about what Jerry was saying. And somehow, for the first time, it made sense. Before, when the scoutmaster had talked about Jesus, and trusting Him, it didn't mean much to Pete. But now it began to fall together. If Jesus had really loved him that much . . . (He could hear Jerry quoting John 3:16 as he thought: "For God so loved the world, that He gave His only begotten son, that whosoever believeth in Him should not perish, but have everlasting life") . . . if Jesus really loved him that much, enough to die for him . . . then, whatever He wanted, Pete decided he'd do it! Then

Jerry's voice came into his consciousness again, and Jerry was saying,

"Do it, Pete, will you? Will you take Him?"

Pete looked at Jerry, there in the waiting room of the hospital, and Jerry thought he had never seen Pete smile before, his face was so different.

"Jerry, I'll do it! If He'll have me, if He loves me that much, then I want to belong to Him! I'll take Him."

Jerry felt so good he didn't know what to say, but he didn't have to say anything, for just at that moment the nurse came in.

"Pardon me," she was saying to Jerry, "But you can see Mr. Spann now. He's in Room 313, at the end of the hall."

Jerry could hardly wait. "C'mon, Pete. We've gotta tell Mr. Spann! Boy, will he be glad to see you!"

It was a happy time around the hospital bed. Jerry was happy to see Mr. Spann again, and happy because he was getting well; and Mr. Spann was happy because Pete had turned to Christ . . . and Pete, well, Pete was just happy about everything.

"Where's Hurry?" Mr. Spann said, when there were a few moments of quiet.

"I don't know," Jerry said. "He was going to come with me, but then he said he had to go to the drug store first. He ought to be here by this time, though."

Just then the door burst open, and Hurry dashed in (much to the disgust of a trim little nurse who was following him, trying vainly to find out which patient he wanted to see.)

"Hi, Mr. Spann. How do you feel?"

"Feel much better, Hurry. Looks like you're going to have to get along with the same old scoutmaster for another year."

"I should think so! We never considered getting another one! Listen, guess what, Jerry and Pete. You got so excited you forgot . . ." and here Hurry waved a copy of the **Post.** . .

"The contest!" said Jerry and Pete at once.

"That's right, this is the day they're announcing the winners, isn't it?" Mr. Spann said. "What does it say, Hurry?"

"Well," Hurry was taking his time, feeling very important . . . "I must say that Whittenburg Scout troop is very well represented. 'The first prize,' it says here, 'goes to a young man named Mr. Peter S. Laughton.'"

Hurry paused a moment to let it sink in. Pete's lips

moved as he whispered to himself, "Fifty dollars!" Jerry's heart sank. No prize for him! But he looked squarely at Pete and said, "Congratulations, Pete!"—and found that he really meant it!

"All right, Hurry. Go ahead." Spann prompted. "What else about the Whittenburg Scout troop?"

"Second prize goes to Mr. Martin T. Whomplesheimer or something—I can't pronounce it—and third prize to— oh, somebody else we don't know. **"But"** and here Hurry's voice took on that important ring again, 'The first honorable mention was won by Mister Jerrold Thomas of Whittenburg'—and Jerry, you get a free week at Photography Camp this summer!"

"Good work, boys," Mr. Spann said. "You aren't too disappointed, are you, Jerry?"

"Nope; I'm glad it was somebody I know that got it. What are you going to do with the $50.00 prize money, Pete?"

Pete was like a different boy. The boldness and the pride were gone, and there was something in his manner completely foreign to his old self.

"I didn't tell you, but just before we moved here I found out my mother was going to have to have an operation . . . Dad didn't have the money and . . . well, I was just hoping I could get the prize for that."

Jerry said, "I'm . . . I'm **really** glad you got it, Pete."

Hurry was looking at Pete as if he were a stranger. "Good night, Pete—we didn't know you were like that!"

Mr. Spann smiled. "That will be a good thing for you to remember, Hurry. Everybody has things inside that you can't see on the outside. That's why it's best to give everyone the benefit of the doubt. And, by the way, Hurry doesn't know about Pete yet. Hurry, Jerry won a reward today, too. And I think it's even better than a fifty dollar reward!"

"Say, didja, Jerry? What is it? Tell me!"

"I'll tell you one thing that happened," Pete said. "I did it—I trusted Jesus, out in the waiting room."

"Aw say, that's swell! But . . . what reward were you talking about, Mr. Spann?"

"He that winneth souls is wise," Mr. Spann said, and they could tell by his voice he was quoting from the Bible. "And they that be wise shall shine as the brightness of the firmament, and they that turn many to righteousness as the stars forever and ever." There were tears in Mr. Spann's eyes as he added, "That's a real reward, Jerry—treasure in Heaven!"